"Why are you be

All at once Laura's heart was beating fast. All wrong, in the circumstances.

"You're a woman on your own, aren't you?" Evan said reasonably. "I'm the kind of man who likes to lend a hand."

"Then I'm very grateful."

"Besides, I've had a good time." He looked at her and gave that white melting smile. "Laura Graham, you scare me." Before he could prevent himself he had touched her cheek lightly with his finger. It had the velvety texture of a magnolia.

For a moment they stared into one another's eyes. Laura felt oddly as if the air might explode. She felt so drawn to him, but she had no doubts that before he'd come to Koomera Crossing he'd been someone very different. She realized that Evan saw her as a vulnerable little rich girl on the run from some demanding boyfriend. She wondered what he would think if she told him the truth.

Dear Reader

Runaway Wife is the story of a sensitive, gifted young woman who marries for love only to find her husband, in public a well-respected surgeon, behind closed doors is an abusive bully who uses any means at his disposal to control her and strip her of all confidence and self-respect. Violence against women is a terrible disease. It knows no boundaries of race, culture or social position.

Our heroine Laura finds the courage to make her escape from an intolerable situation. She flees to the Outback where, with the help of an ally, Dr Sarah Dempsey of the Koomera Crossing Bush Hospital, she sets about taking the first steps towards rehabilitation.

In this remote Outback town her destiny becomes powerfully entwined with that of mystery man Evan Thompson. Evan too bears terrible scars. He has come to the Outback to heal. Together Laura and Evan forge the most vital emotional connection of all. They fall in love. But first Laura has to overcome her great battle with past fears and humiliations to lay her trust at Evan's door. Only in doing so can she begin the process of facing up to her husband and reconstructing her life.

The first book in my **Koomera Crossing** mini-series was *Sarah's Baby*. Look for Christine's story, coming soon.

Margaret Way

RUNAWAY WIFE

BY
MARGARET WAY

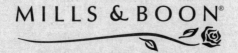

*All the characters in this book have no existence outside the imagination
of the author, and have no relation whatsoever to anyone bearing the
same name or names. They are not even distantly inspired by any
individual known or unknown to the author, and all the incidents are
pure invention.*

*First published in Great Britain 2003
Harlequin Mills & Boon Limited,
Eton House, 18-24 Paradise Road, Richmond, Surrey TW9 1SR*

© Margaret Way Pty., Ltd. 2003

ISBN 0 263 83388 7

*Set in Times Roman 10 on 10¾ pt.
02-0803-54680*

*Printed and bound in Spain
by Litografia Rosés, S.A., Barcelona*

PROLOGUE

SHE never felt safe any more. Not living with Colin. Though she struggled to live normally, the truth was she was frightened all the time. Laura knew all the signs. Emotional and physical exhaustion, trembling limbs, fluttery pulse, sick panic inside her.

After another of Colin's irrational and unprovoked attacks on her the previous night, she knew she had to go somewhere he would never find her. She had to make a decision and stick with it. She had to reclaim herself, her body, her mind, her drastically fractured self-esteem. Reared gently by loving parents, she found Colin's behaviour entirely incomprehensible.

Since their big society marriage almost a year before, reality had become a far cry from their public image of glamorous, affluent couple. The thrill of being married had died before it had ever begun. Their marriage was a nightmare. Her dream of a happy partnership, of security, children, shattered.

Her brilliant young husband, a rising star in open-heart surgery, had turned out to be dangerously unstable—though such was his public persona no one who knew him would ever have guessed. His mother, maybe? Laura had always thought Sonia Morcombe recognised her son had a dark side, but instinctively chose to ignore it. It was easier that way. After all Colin was brilliant in every other way. Respected in his profession.

But the much-admired Colin had taught his bride not to love but to fear him. Because of his unpredictable moods, his sexual demands, his never-ending put-downs and profound jealousies, he had lost her love. Most certainly he had lost her most of her friends, subtly isolating her from anyone who

5

was smart and confident and might help her. She saw far less of everyone.

Her music was out. He had forbidden her to continue with her studies. It was his role to "take care" of her, to make all her decisions for her. Clever, manipulative, psychotic Colin. He acted as though it had been ordained from On High he would occupy the central position in her life. She would rely on him for her every want, her every need. He lived to possess her.

After every terrifying outburst of rage, while the tears rolled down her cheeks, he insisted he loved her dearly. The fault lay in her. For a while he'd had her believing she wasn't a real woman at all. He blamed her pampered upbringing for what she was now. Pathetic. He was sick to death of hearing about her father, the special closeness they shared. It had obviously been an unhealthy fixation.

"Daddy's little girl!"

The way he said it, so contemptuous and scathing, hurt her terribly but it could not dim her loving memories of her father. Her father, unlike Colin, had been a man who inspired love. Not Colin. He reminded her constantly *he* was the brilliant one, the man who saved lives. The best she could do was play the piano. What sort of a job was that?

She couldn't hold a decent conversation. Compared to him she was relatively uneducated. An "unsophisticated nothing" before he married her. A pretty object he'd bought and paid for. If she'd acquired any polish it was through him.

"You'll never leave me, Laura," he assured her, his voice deadly quiet. "You wouldn't know how to function on your own. You need me to survive."

She knew perfectly well it was a warning. She wished she was stronger, but she wasn't. She hadn't had enough life experience. She felt more as if she was fragmenting into little pieces.

There were a good many ways of expressing love. Flinging her up against walls with one violent sweep of the arm wasn't one of them. Neither was insatiable lovemaking so rough she cried out in pain.

Up until last night Colin had taken good care not to damage her face. The face he "adored". He'd actually said that. She had a sickening image of him standing over her, expression enraged, as she huddled on the floor, her arms wrapped protectively around her body.

Colin was a slim man but very fit, an inch under six feet. She was a light-boned five-three, her body weight constantly dropping as she lost appetite. She had learned from her beautiful, gracious mother how to be a good cook, a good hostess, a good homemaker, but Colin had never been satisfied with her. There was no way she could please him. Not even in bed, which was crazy, because he couldn't get enough of her. Sex, too, was a way of controlling her.

"Just as well you're beautiful, Laura," he'd taunted her, and she was too hurting, too demoralized to fight back. "Because you're bloody useless in bed. You don't know the first thing about pleasing a man. You need to get out a few books. You act so guilty you're like some frigid little nun."

She was frigid now. With him. Mentally and emotionally removing herself as much as she possibly could from the act. Was this marriage, or rape? She felt demeaned, defiled, humiliated beyond all telling, her mind bent on strategies for escape even as she lived with the underlying fear he would find her wherever she went.

Laura realized with dread she knew her strange husband better than anyone, outside his mother, who would probably defend her son to the death.

They'd met by chance. Overnight the whole tenor of her quiet, studious life had changed. He had bombarded her with attention: fine restaurants, red roses, chocolates, champagne, books he wanted her to read—he never read them himself. He was so charming, so attentive, so handsome and cultured, and their romance had flowered.

She had realized too late she was simply filling the deep void left by the premature death of her beloved father in a road accident when she was seventeen.

The stage had been set. She'd ceded him power. A virgin still, because she'd wanted to be absolutely sure she was giving herself to someone she loved and who loved her, she'd been ridiculously high-minded. She thought of herself now as having been incredibly naïve.

She'd been studying classical piano—very motivated, self-disciplined, a born musician. Her parents had always been so proud of her and her accomplishment. She'd worked hard to give something back to them.

Her father's death had been a tremendous blow to her and her mother, striking grief into their souls. She'd been an only child, living a near idyllic existence.

She grew up overnight.

Strangely, her mother had adjusted to their loss much more quickly than she had. Her mother had confided she couldn't face life being alone. She'd had one happy marriage, a marvellous partner. She desired another. It wasn't a betrayal of Laura's father. She had his memory locked away in her heart. It was a recognition of the great joys a happy marriage could bring.

Her mother had eventually found a good, caring man, a fellow guest at a wedding. Six months later her mother had married her sheep farmer and gone to settle with her new husband in the South Island of New Zealand, a most beautiful part of the world.

Laura had stayed behind, though they'd both wanted her to join them. Laura believed the marriage would develop better if her mother and her new husband were left alone. She could always visit.

She'd already graduated from the Conservatorium and started on a Doctorate of Music at the university. She'd taken private pupils as well, for experience and to supplement her income—though her father had left her and her mother well provided for. Her father had been absolutely wonderful. She'd had to struggle to survive without him. And she'd been struggling ever since.

She hadn't taken a fine man like her father for a husband. She had taken Colin, a man with serious problems, a man who took pleasure in hurting her.

The first time she'd met him was at a concert given by a

visiting piano virtuoso, a wonderfully gifted woman who really made the keyboard sound. Colin had remarked in a patronising aside that no woman pianist could ever hope to match a man. She should have told him he'd do better to stick to surgery, where he could play God. Colin, the dyed-in-the-wool chauvinist. She should have been warned then.

As chance or malign fate had it, they'd each attended the concert on their own. She and a girlfriend had had tickets, but her friend had had to cancel at the last minute through sickness. In the intermission Colin had shifted in his seat to seek her opinion, smiling with open pleasure and admiration into her eyes. He had suggested a glass of champagne in the foyer.

It was the first time ever she'd allowed herself to be "picked up", as she thought of it, but he had seemed eminently respectable, especially when he'd told her he was a doctor from a well-known medical family.

After the performance they had gone on to have coffee at a popular night spot. There she had opened up as she'd never done before. She had been lonely. That was the reason. Still cast as the beloved, indulged only child at twenty-two. Her life, in a sense, had been cloistered.

She recognised it all now. She'd been in a very vulnerable situation, badly missing her mother and father. Colin had seemed so sympathetic. She supposed because of her father she gravitated towards older men. Also Colin loved music, which she had intended to make her profession.

She soon learned Colin had only pretended to love music. In actual fact it meant little to him. A friend had given him the ticket. At a rare loose end, he had decided to go along. He was a man of culture after all. That was the image he liked to project.

Their meeting, he told her exhaustively, had been destiny. She had been there waiting for him to come and carry her off to a new life together. She'd thought he meant they were perfectly matched. She couldn't count the number of times he'd told her she looked beautiful. Before their marriage.

"Your long gleaming dark hair, your green eyes, white skin! The gentle haunting beauty I admire above all!"

What he had really been saying was he thought she would be not only easy to control, but exquisite to torment.

If only she'd been older. Had known more about life. If only her father had lived. If only her mother hadn't remarried and gone away. The endless ifs.

She hadn't been ready for commitment. She'd needed a little time. But Colin had swept her off her feet. He was already in his early thirties, which he perceived as exactly the right age for a man to marry. She was an innocent ten years his junior.

Colin had accomplished their whirlwind engagement within three months. His parents—she'd had to hide from herself the fact she couldn't like them—seemed to recognise she was the sort of young woman their adored son wanted. Someone he could dominate. Certainly someone who would look up to him and allow herself to be moulded by his hand.

Her mother and stepfather had journeyed from New Zealand to meet Colin a scant fortnight before the wedding. Her mother had been genuinely delighted with her prospective son-in-law. Colin had gone all out to be charming. Craig hadn't been quite so forthcoming, simply saying it was very obvious Colin was "very much in love with his lovely, gifted, fiancée."

The wedding had been lavish. The planning having been taken out of her control by Sonia Morcombe. Their whole future had stretched ahead of them.

The abuse had started on their honeymoon, profoundly shocking her. She'd gone into a stupefied withdrawal, wondering if she was going to end up dead when all he seemed to want to do was take her to bed.

She mustn't flirt with every man she met. She mustn't be provocative in her conversation. She mustn't smile and tilt her head, so. The accusations had never finished; his temper had snapped so easily. She had been overwhelmed by terror and—incredibly—remorse. Maybe she *was* being unconsciously provocative? Maybe she *was* doing what he was saying?

She knew she was attractive to men. Her looks had seen to that. Even her girlfriend, Ellie, teased her endlessly about her "certain smile". "What a come-on, Laura!"

She, herself, was at a loss to know why.

"You're my wife, Laura. Mine," Colin always told her as he delivered another hard lesson. "I won't tolerate your coy glances elsewhere."

An hour after the abuse stopped he was cordial, composed, even tender. She could never believe it was the same man. He acted as though nothing disturbing had happened. It was simply that it was a man's right to chastise his wife. It was the only way she would ever learn.

So, on her honeymoon her marriage had taken a giant leap backwards. Even as she had strived to please him she had despised herself for not standing up for her rights. How could he say he loved her when a lot of the time he acted as though he hated her? She hadn't known where to turn. Her father would never have allowed this situation. But her father had gone. In truth she had felt orphaned, utterly defeated, down.

There wasn't going to be any pitter-patter of tiny feet either. Not for a good long time.

"We're happy just the two of us!"

From his laugh and the light in his cold grey eyes it had sounded as though he believed it.

Now she had to escape. It wouldn't be simple, but she had thought it through. She couldn't continue to allow Colin to abuse her. She had to reach safety.

She'd made one previous attempt, seeking the aid of a girlfriend, but Colin had quickly convinced her friend she was experiencing "problems". He was a doctor, after all. But now she was ready.

She was frustrated by the fact she simply couldn't move out of the house and take an apartment somewhere. She knew Colin would find her. Teach her a lesson with his clever, damaging hands. Part of her even believed he might kill her if she expressed her fervent desire to be free of him. She had to go so far away it would be difficult to trace her.

She already knew the place. Koomera Crossing in far Western Queensland. There could be nowhere more remote than the Outback. She knew the name of a woman who might help her cope with the crippling fear she'd been living with. An absolutely steady woman who'd impressed her every time they'd met. A woman not all that much older than herself. Highly intelligent, caring, a doctor now in charge of the Koomera Crossing Bush Hospital.

Her name was Sarah Dempsey. Laura had met Sarah many times at various functions she and Colin had attended in their role of ''perfect'' couple. Laura had formed the opinion Sarah Dempsey was a strong, supportive woman, unusually kind and sensitive. The sort of woman who might help her win back her life. Or at least provide the safety net she desperately needed until she felt strong enough to stand on her own two feet.

CHAPTER ONE

SARAH had given her a list of three rental houses that were available in the town. She could make her own choice. It was Sarah who had come along to pick out the reliable used car she was driving. She could have bought a new one from the considerable cash stash she had with her, withdrawn from her private account, but she didn't want to draw too much attention to herself. Sarah had helped immensely by introducing her around as an ''old friend''. It had instantly assured her acceptance in the town.

In the course of a few days Sarah had become her friend and confidante. A sister in arms. Laura knew from the moment she'd laid eyes on Dr Sarah at the hospital she'd made the right decision finding her way to Koomera Crossing. Simply by talking over her sad situation with someone who seemed eminently qualified to listen and offer strategies for change had made her feel so much better about herself.

Laura felt reasonably normal, though she never lost the feeling of being in jeopardy, or visualizing Colin's angry face many times a day. She knew with a certainty Colin would have begun tracking her, most probably through some investigation agency, but she'd been surprisingly adept at getting away. How had she allowed him to make her feel so incompetent when all her life up to that point she'd been regarded as very bright? Such was the pain-inducing power of the domineering male.

Now, with Sarah's help, she was beginning to stop blaming herself for the disastrous failure of her marriage. She was beginning to see Colin had worked so hard to instill in her a sense of worthlessness he had almost succeeded. Sarah's opinion of Colin as a sociopath, a condition in which he considered himself beyond the normal rules, was that he was the one who truly needed counselling.

13

Laura was young, inexperienced, grieving for her father, lonely for her mother—ill-prepared to cope with a man like Colin Morcombe with his anger and aggressions.

As soon as she felt stronger and more confident Sarah would encourage her to do something about her situation. Liberate herself from Colin and the bonds he had forced on her. Divorce him and change her life.

It sounded simple but Laura, the victim, like all other victims of abuse, knew it wasn't. She had suffered far too much emotional damage living with Colin, but she wasn't beyond repair. Though Colin had tried so very hard to break her she had found the strength to make her escape.

But for how long? Colin would come after her. Hadn't he near convinced her there was no way out?

All this Laura thought as she drove around the town, looking for the best place to live. Koomera Crossing boasted a picture-postcard town. It was very neat and clean with a lot of picturesque colonial buildings, but the majority of the houses she drove past were humble compared with what she'd been used to.

Her own family home, the house where she had grown up, now sold to family friends who had always admired it, was a gracious "Queenlander", set in a large garden, a luxurious tropical oasis, that had been her mother's pride and joy.

Laura and Colin had lived in a starkly modern edifice— she'd never thought of it as "home"—with a commanding view of the river and the city. An architect friend of Colin's had designed it. There had been much talk of clean, open spaces, energy flow and creative processes—about which, for all the notice they took of her, she knew nothing. When she had attempted to say what she liked both men had shrugged her and her opinions off. The client was Colin. Not his wife. Her needs—warmth, colour, comfort—were just too "precious". Traditional was out. What they got, to Colin's delight, was a massive white pile. Geometric and pompous.

"Let's keep the whole thing white," Colin had suggested, as though she had any say in the matter. "Inside and out. You have to think modern, darling. Not that *Gone With the*

Wind old barn you came from. Try to look happier. Most women would be very excited about living in our house. If you want a bit of colour you can get it from steel and glass. Glass has a beautiful blue-green edge.''

The houses she was driving past, cottages with tiny porches, would have fitted comfortably into their living room, with its giant sofas and huge abstract paintings—mostly black, silver or charcoal on white.

"Challenging," Colin had said, the self-deluded art connoisseur.

"Why do we need a living room so big?" she'd been brave enough to ask.

"For entertaining, you silly goose. That's if you ever become confident enough to try it."

They rarely had entertained.

"You poor kid, stuck with this!" her friend, Ellie had said, giving the interior a quick, assessing look. "Gee, after what you came from you must be finding all this very different?"

"Challenging." She'd laughed with good humour, giving an excellent imitation of Colin's ultra-confident tones.

She knew Ellie wouldn't have been fooled. Ellie was a very independent person, very sure of herself. She held her own with Colin. Needless to say Ellie had been one of the first to be struck from the list.

Laura wasn't concerned where she'd be living now, as long as it was clean and safe.

Twenty minutes later she decided where she wanted to live. It was a modest dwelling, by far the smallest in the street. She supposed it had originally been a settlers' cottage, constructed of timber and corrugated iron with a small front verandah to keep off the powerful glare of the sun and the rain. She had to wonder just how often it rained out here on the desert fringe.

The cottage was painted white, with sunshine-yellow shutters and trim. It was surrounded by a low picket fence hung with masses of Thai Gold bougainvillaea in abundant flower, giving the place a delightful welcoming look. Whoever had lived in it previously had maintained a pocket handkerchief cottage garden filled with bright yellow and white paper daisy flowers and a dazzling blanket of waxy pink flowers with sparkly silver-pale green leaves backed by tall, rather regal-looking lilies, the heraldic cream and orange blooms swaying slightly in the breeze.

There didn't appear to be anywhere to garage the car. Indeed, the whole cottage wasn't as big as the six-car garage Colin had insisted upon to house his collection of classic cars and her Volvo. A safe car for a ''truly dreadful driver''. She'd soon stopped driving Colin anywhere because he heckled her so much. It had been equally grim in the kitchen, where he'd told her constantly she'd never make a living as a chef.

She remembered the first and the last time she had told him to shut up, and felt instantly ashamed she hadn't left him there and then.

So what had their marriage been? Sex? For someone who found her frigid he had spent a lot of time taking her to bed.

Laura got out of the car, keys to the cottage in hand. She didn't look closely at the houses to either side, wondering if she was under surveillance. One was a high-set colonial, far grander than the cottages, its grounds immaculate and studded with palms.

The picket gate swung cleanly without a creak. She closed it after her carefully, looking around with quiet pleasure at the small garden as though it was already hers to put to order. It was beginning to encroach on the narrow paved path up to the two weather-worn steps that led to the verandah.

The key fitted neatly into the lock. She opened the yellow-painted timber door with its old brass knocker and stepped inside, feeling a little Alice in Wonderland full of wonder with her curiosity to explore.

A hallway with a polished floor, pale golden wood with a darker grained border, ran straight through the house to the rear door. She wandered from room to room peering in. Parlour to the left, dining room, to the right. Beyond the parlour a fair-sized bedroom which led to a very quaint bathroom; behind the small dining room an equally small kitchen, somewhat modernized with a curved banquette area. Five rooms in all. No laundry. Unless there was one outside.

There was. It was attached to the cottage by a covered walkway hung with a glorious bridal veil of white bougainvillaea. Laura walked out into the sun. It was so brilliantly golden she needed her sunglasses or she'd be dazzled.

Another cottage garden, even more overgrown. It curved away to either side of a pink brick path that drew her along. Masses and masses of lavender gone wild. She picked a sprig, waved it beneath her nose. The path disappeared into a tunnel of lantana, flowering monstrously, richly blazing orange. There was even a small, charming bird bath, though the bowl was cracked.

This place is mine. It's wonderful! Laura, who had grown up with every possible comfort, breathed aloud. A doll's house.

She wandered back along the path to sit down on the hot stone step, lifting her arms as if in praise of the sun. She was drawing out every moment of the peace and freedom she had been denied living with Colin. The aromatic scents of the garden and the great wilderness that lay just beyond the town were balm to her wounded heart.

"Please God, help me," she prayed. "I can't hide for ever."

There were no furnishings. She told herself she didn't need much. She even felt a tingle of anticipation at the idea of making the cottage comfortable. And her own. She knew intellectually she was going to ground. Emotionally she felt if she didn't hide away she was risking her life, and there were frightening statistics to back her fears. A wife-abuser was unpredictable and dangerous.

I'm in the middle of nowhere, she thought with a tremendous sense of relief. Who could find me here in this vast landscape, so stunningly, wonderfully primitive, as though nothing has changed for countless thousands of years?

She had fallen in love with the Outback town, a small settlement on the desert fringe. Beyond the town's ordered perimeters lay the wild bush. What she had seen of its unique

beauty had cast a compulsive spell on her. The amazing colours! The deep fiery red of the earth and the extraordinary
rock formations; the breathtaking cobalt blue of the cloudless
sky that contrasted so vividly with the blood-red soil; the
myriad greens and silver-greens of the wild bush and the
iridescent greens of the countless creeks and billabongs that
criss-crossed the huge area.

There was such a feeling of space and freedom she was
beginning to feel a difference in herself. She was less upset,
less disturbed, less fearful. She had taken the first big step to
help herself. She could take another if she kept to the fore-
front of her mind that a journey of a thousand miles began
with the very first step. She could be what she was meant to
be—a woman who had confidence in her own ability to look
after herself. A woman who cared about others. A woman
who took delight in friendships and her once deeply satisfying talent.

She could start again. That meant at some point divorcing
Colin, but first she would have to bring about changes in
herself. She had to grow and learn, see herself as someone
who could handle life's difficulties. She had to stop for ever
looking over her shoulder, as though she expected to see
Colin, his arm outstretched to grab her. She had to subdue
and conquer her fear of Colin.

She knew one day, perhaps sooner than she thought, she
would be free.

Drawing her long hair over her shoulder, Laura walked
back inside the cottage. She had already decided she would
take it, and her mind was busy with thoughts of exactly how
much furniture she would need. What would go where? Her
enthusiasm for this little cottage in the back of beyond was
infectious. In fact she felt quite jubilant. It was a long long
time since she'd felt that.

Laura took a little notebook out of her shoulder bag and
began to scribble in it.

CHAPTER TWO

THE sound of a car door slamming broke his concentration. Not that the book was going so well at this point. Memories always made him suffer. Writing kept him sane.

In this little Outback town of Koomera Crossing he was known as Evan Thompson. Loner. Man of mystery. He'd had an ironic laugh at those names. Evan Thompson wasn't his true identity. It was a cover of sorts for his secret life as a wood worker. He'd had no apprenticeship in the trade. He'd learned in his youth from his diplomat father, who'd channelled his abundant natural skills into an avenue for relaxation.

His father! Christian Kellerman. Killed in a terrorist attack in the Balkans.

In another life he'd been known as Evan Kellerman, respected foreign correspondent, who had earned a reputation for putting his own life on the line to get to a big story. Everything he had written from the war zones where he'd gone searching for truthful answers had had an insider's knowledge. With a base in Vienna, close to his father, he had covered the war in the Balkans when three ethnic groups had been at each other's throats. Even after the Dayton Peace Agreement he had stayed on to cover the demilitarisation.

He had had a story to tell. Not the usual coverage of the war and recent political developments, but one man's day-to-day existence during that violent time, when he had been plunged into a world gone mad and a journalist's life was greatly at risk.

The terror had taken his father and an alluring but traitorous woman. Monika Reiner. Evan's lover. So-called patriot. But Monika, unknown to him and his associates, had had an agenda of her own. Spying for the enemy.

Monika Reiner had used her beauty and her useful contacts

19

to infiltrate the ranks of freedom fighters, leaving behind her a trail of death. All in the name of greed, money and power. And to think such a woman, responsible for passing on his father's itinerary on that terrible day, had held the key to his heart. The sense of guilt, though irrational, had almost destroyed him.

He stood up so precipitately he sent his swivel chair flying. After a minute he retrieved it, but he couldn't return to his desk. Restlessly he prowled, like a wild animal in a cage. From a bedroom window he caught sight of the young woman who must have slammed her car door. She was going into the cottage next door.

He shifted the curtain a fraction, looking down into the neighbouring garden. She was walking slowly, almost drifting in the breeze. His heart suddenly kicked in his chest. He sucked in his breath, momentarily overcome by paralysing shock.

From this distance she looked like Monika. Graceful in body and movement. Almost feline.

She was beautiful too, with long flowing dark hair that lifted away from her face as the breeze caught it. Like Monika's, her hair was center-parted. She was petite, very slender. He could see her luminous white skin. He found his hands clenching and unclenching as he was gripped by the past.

"Close your eyes with holy dread." The words of a poet sprang instantly into his mind.

He swallowed on a dry throat, turning away abruptly. A passing resemblance. Nothing more. A figure type.

He walked purposefully to the kitchen to make himself some strong black coffee. As soon as he finished his book—he was more than halfway through it—he would try to get back to a normal life. Or as normal as he could manage after the hell he'd been through.

Evan knew he could have his career back tomorrow. To this day he was being pursued by various agencies who well remembered his "meritorious service"—but he didn't know if he could live that life again, with the sound of gunfire forever reverberating through his head. The Outback, the Timeless Land, had offered solace, a place to write and lick his wounds.

He found himself moving to the rear closed-in verandah, steaming coffee cup in hand, to check on the girl.

There she was again, turned flower child, twirling a sprig of lavender beneath her nose. He could have moved off, but the sight of her halted and held him. She looked so innocent as she walked among the blossoms, admiring the pretty petals.

He knew the cottage was up for rent. His neighbours, the Lawsons, had gone back to the UK for a year or two to be with family. Surely this young woman didn't intend to live there? Everything about her—the lustrous hair, the trendy clothes, the graceful limbs—carried the stamp of "money", or at the very least a comfortable background. What would she be doing looking over a modest little cottage in an Outback town?

Very odd! Even odder was the way she was taking such pleasure in the tiny backyard that had run riot since the Lawsons had left. He was disconcerted by his reaction to her beauty and her slightly fey attitude. What the hell was the matter with her? She was treading the path rather vaguely, picking wildflowers, but looking so utterly captivating she might have been modelling for a photo shoot.

I don't need this, he thought. I definitely don't need this. Beauty was a bait to lure. Yet he didn't move, scarcely aware the coffee cup was burning his hand.

He couldn't put his finger on just why he thought there was something disturbed or disturbing about this girl. Instinct again. His instincts were significant. They had saved his life time and time again—though that made him feel guilty he had survived when others so close to him had not.

Butterflies were fluttering around the lantana. A magical sight. She was looking towards it in an apparent trance of beauty. He felt an involuntary hostility well up in him. Simply because something about her had reminded him of

Monika? This girl was a total stranger. She could never have witnessed an ugly sight in her life.

She strolled back along the path, taking a seat on the stone step. This wasn't wise, watching her, but still he remained. Again she surprised him, raising her slender arms gracefully, dramatically, to the blue sky like some sort of ritual to the sun.

Bravo! A would-be ballerina! He kept his gaze focused. Perhaps she'd guessed she had an audience? She certainly couldn't see him from where he stood.

"There's more to this woman than meets the eye!"

He was surprised he'd spoken aloud, but the words had flowed irresistibly. He couldn't believe he was even doing this. Spying on a perfect stranger. Normally he guarded his privacy and isolation.

With one exception. Harriet Crompton, the town school teacher and a character in her own right.

He had taken a liking to Harriet to the extent that he had agreed, after some heavy persuasion, to join the town orchestra, and then make up a surprisingly good quartet. He played cello. Harriet played viola. His mother, a concert artist, had taught him first the piano and then, when his interest had waned, the cello from an early age. He hadn't wanted to make music his career—he had far too many interests—but that hadn't prevented him from becoming very proficient. He guessed, as his mother always said, music ran in his blood.

These days it could make him very unhappy. He couldn't listen to certain great artists for very long. Those who played with great passion, like the tragic Jacqueline Du Pré. It almost brought him to despair. He'd thought he had put his journalistic talents to the advancement of a downtrodden people and their cause. All it had brought about was the death of a father he had rightfully idolized and a profound mistrust of beautiful women.

Like the young woman who had disappeared back inside the cottage.

Ten minutes later and she still hadn't come out. What was she doing?

By that stage he was back to his prowling. He knew the house was unfurnished. The Lawsons had preferred to store their furniture—a lot of genuine colonial pieces. He returned to his desk, but such was his mood he made the unprecedented decision to go next door and ask the young woman one or two questions.

He couldn't explain the need to do so to himself beyond the fact his instincts were exceptionally finely honed. They told him she brought trouble. Or trouble was reaching out for her. One or the other.

He didn't spend any more time thinking about it. He obeyed the powerful urge.

The brightly painted front door was open. An invitation? He gave a couple of raps. That should bring her.

Maybe, just maybe, she looked nothing like Monika beyond the white skin and the long waterfall of dark hair. He had spent a long time thinking about Monika and her treachery, which had ultimately cost his father and his father's driver their lives.

His hand on the doorjamb was registering a faint tremor. Some things he couldn't banish.

He'd realized at some time someone would rent the cottage. He'd hoped for a quiet couple. The sudden appearance of the girl had shocked him out of his complacency. He didn't want her close. The wrong time. The wrong place. A random visit? Fate?

He heard her light footsteps, then she rounded the corner of the dining room, a half-smile on her face as though she expected someone. A friend? Her eyes—a beautiful iridescent green—at first radiant, suddenly flooded with something he interpreted instantly as panic. He knew all about panic. He couldn't be fooled.

How very damned odd! Why should she look so shaken? He wasn't that formidable, was he? Although he'd been told many times he was.

He damned nearly gave his real name—he was only trying to project reassurance. But he didn't move an inch from the door, all at once wanting to release her from her high tension.

He hadn't considered she would have that effect on him. He had no wish to frighten her, and frighten her he had.

"Evan Thompson. I live next door," he gestured with his hand. "The colonial." In the space of about a minute she haunted his eyes.

"Laura...Graham." She responded so hesitantly it immediately spun into his mind that it wasn't her real name any more than his was Thompson.

Laura, in turn, realized within the space of a second that this was the fascinating "loner" Harriet had told her about.

"I'm sorry if I startled you." He was aware his apology was overly clipped and formal. But he couldn't seem to stop looking at her. The long dark hair, the white skin, the delicate bone structure and petite stature. Otherwise she was nothing like Monika.

Monika had had gold unwinking eyes, like a cat's. Monika had never looked frightened—even when the game was up and she'd been surrounded by the comrades of the patriots she'd betrayed. Men about to pass instant judgement and there had been no way he could have stopped them.

Laura said nothing for a moment, aware she was under intense scrutiny. "I wasn't expecting a man at my door," she explained.

He answered dryly. "I'll go if you prefer."

"Oh, no!" She half raised a hand, let it drop. "I'm sorry. I must sound flustered."

"One wonders why. I'm not that frightening, am I?"

She studied him, thinking Harriet's description had been excellent. Late thirties. Exceptionally handsome in a dark, brooding way. Deep resonant voice. Thick dark hair. Brilliant dark eyes. Heavy sculptured head. A big man, strongly built.

She sensed he was somehow hostile to women. To her? That didn't make sense.

Grooves ran from his nose to his mouth, bracketing it and drawing attention to its chiselled perfection. A sensuous mouth. A contradiction.

"Not at all!" She tried hard to suppress her agitation, knowing colour was running beneath her skin. "I thought it was someone else. Someone who knows I'm here, inspecting the house.''

''You like it?''

''I do.''

He regarded her lovely face, clear of that early expression of panic. ''May I ask if you intend to rent it?''

''I don't think I could if I had to get your approval,'' She read his mind.

''On the contrary, I don't care who moves in as long as they're quiet. May I enquire too if you'll be on your own?'' He couldn't keep the sardonic note out of his voice.

She stared back at him, trying to formulate an answer. He was formidable, but not threatening. Experienced. Tough. But never the sort of man to lift his hand in anger to a woman. Such a thing would only rouse in him revulsion. All this she saw even as she registered he would be very difficult to know. Very complex.

''It's not a crime, is it?''

''It is if you play pop music very loudly.'' Unexpectedly he smiled, sunlight from behind storm clouds.''

''I don't know much about pop music at all,'' she confessed, lulled by that smile. ''I'm a classically trained pianist without a piano. I expect you'll be grateful for that.''

''Not at all. I grew up in a house of music. My mother is a cellist.''

''Would I know of her?'' she asked with genuine interest.

''Could be.'' He looked away.

''I thought I might have a career as a pianist,'' she found herself confiding.

''So what happened?''

''It didn't work out.'' She too changed the subject. ''I'm a friend of Sarah Dempsey, by the way.'' She said it as though Sarah's name could offer safety and acceptance.

''She's a very beautiful woman and a fine doctor. The town counts itself lucky to have her. I've met Dr Dempsey, most notably at her engagement party. I know her fiancé Kyall McQueen better. All in all they're an extraordinary couple. You and Sarah were at school together? No, what made me say that? You'd be some years younger..."

"It's not how old you are, it's how old you feel," she found herself saying dangerously.

"Really? And how do you feel, Miss Graham?"

"As though I'm being quietly interrogated." She met the darkness of his eyes.

"'Quietly' and 'interrogated' are mutually exclusive."

"You sound as if you know. Have you been in the Forces at some time? Secret Intelligence Service?" She was only half joking. Undeniably he had that sort of presence. Even standing perfectly still he give the impression he was at high alert, ready, engines running.

"I wonder how you ever thought that?" he answered smoothly, though her observation had thrown him.

"Am I right or wrong?"

"You couldn't be more wrong." He grimaced. "I'm a humble wood worker."

"You surely don't think yourself humble?" What was the matter with her? She was breaking all the rules.

"All right, then, you tell me?"

"I think you're a casualty of battle." My God had she said that?

He raised a large, sculpted hand. " Miss Graham, you've blown my cover."

"Sometimes an emotional response can be quite unconnected to appearance or reason."

"I just happen to agree." Out of nowhere a complex intimacy was taking hold. "If you think you know something of me, may I ask if in coming out here to the desert you're making a fresh start?"

His voice was deliberately bland, but it didn't fool Laura. "I've made you angry."

"You've thrown down a challenge. That's different." When she had cut through his barriers with frightening ease. Few people had ever done that. Even hardened professionals.

"I won't bother you, Mr Thompson, if that's what you're worried about."

"When you're the sort of woman who would always bother a man?" His watchful eye caught her tremble. "Forgive me. I'm quite sure we're going to be good neighbours as long as we keep to 'good morning' and 'good evening' over the fence. That's if you're going to stay?"

"Unfortunately, yes." She gave him a tiny smile.

"I'm quite sure it's not what you're used to."

"No more than you, in the old colonial next door. Actually, I was making some notes about what sort of furniture I'd need when you knocked."

"There's a good secondhand store in the main street," he found himself telling her. "The cottage is sound structurally. You'll need the fireplace from time to time. Desert nights can get very cold. Is this in the nature of a breathing space? Don't you have people who will miss you?"

"My life can wait.' She didn't attempt to say it lightly. He wouldn't be fooled. "As for you? Don't you have a story to tell?"

"I suppose I should ask are you psychic?" His voice was deliberately dry. "You have a witch's beautiful green eyes. Surely a give-away. Then again, you could be a spoilt little rich girl on the run."

She visibly paled. "And if I were you wouldn't protect me?"

He was silent for a moment, her words and that spontaneous intimacy hammering away at him. "We'll deal with that when the time comes. You need have no fear of me, Miss Graham. I don't know who you are, but I do know you're taking a risk."

"Is it possible you're psychic yourself? You know nothing whatever about me."

"Quite possibly I'm like you." He shrugged. "Covering my tracks. I'll keep quiet if you will."

She watched him, watching her. "How did this all start?" she asked genuinely taken aback. "I don't understand how we got into this conversation at all." For all its curious liberation.

"I do," he said with surprising gentleness. "Sometimes it happens like that. A shortcut to discovery."

"It strikes me as very strange, all the same."

"Have no fears. Though when I saw you in the garden I thought fear would be alien to you. You looked so innocent, I suppose."

"So why have you changed your mind?"

"You're too intense, and there's a haunting in your eyes."

"All right, you're a psychiatrist?" She tried to cover her confusion with a banter. "A highbrow writer? Award-winning journalist? You're very intense too."

"That comes with things we have to guard."

"Then both of us have been very revealing this morning," she said. Certainly nothing like this had ever happened to her before.

"It would seem so. I don't often meet a young woman so disconcertingly perceptive. Also, you're something of an enigma. You're too young to have had much life experience? How old? Twenty-one, twenty-two?" His eyes dipped from her face to take in her slender body in cool white skirt and ruffled top, a mix of cotton and lace. Refined. Virginal.

"Can you deal with twenty-three?" He was clearly much older, with a wealth of experience behind those dark eyes.

"A baby," he concluded.

"I don't think so." Her fingers clenched white. She was quite old enough to have had bad experiences.

He didn't miss the movement of her fingers. "You know about tragedy?"

"Tragedy spills into lots of people's lives. Maybe not on the level of what happened to you. What did happen to you?" she asked after a pause.

"Miss Graham, I'd have to know you a whole lot better before you could ever make that breakthrough," he answered sardonically. "Besides, I'm pretty sure you're not willing to tell *your* story."

"Investigative reporter? Something tells me I should know you." He had far too much presence to be an ordinary everyday person.

"You don't," he assured her briskly. "Anyway, we're not adversaries. Are we?"

"I hope not, Mr Thompson. It'll be a whole lot safer to be on your side."

"You amaze me," he offered freely. And she did.

"*You* amaze *me*," she admitted in wry surprise. "I hadn't bargained on more than a brief introduction. Are you always like this with strangers?"

"You're not a stranger," he said, with a dismissive shrug of his powerful shoulders. "I hadn't bargained on liking you either."

"Ah, so I wasn't wrong. I could feel the hostility when you first arrived."

"You assumed that," he corrected.

"No. It's true."

"All right," he shrugged. "For a few moments you reminded me of someone I used to know."

"Someone no longer in your life?" At his expression her smile faded.

"Exactly." The brilliant dark eyes became hooded. "Anyway, apart from a few similarities you're not like her at all."

"That's good. You had me worried until you smiled."

"That's it? A smile?" he questioned, with a faint twist of his mouth.

"Yes," she said simply, almost with relief. She didn't add that as a big man he was in such possession of the space around him. Necessarily the dominant male. Colin had lacked this man's presence, for all her husband's arrogance and physical attributes. How she wished her life had gone otherwise.

Poignancy left its imprint on her face. Women like her always made a man protective, Evan thought. "Well, I've got an hour or two to kill," he found himself saying. "Would you like some help picking out furniture?"

"You mean you accept me as your neighbour?" Her eyes lit up.

"I accept that in some way you're very vulnerable."

"You're accustomed to vulnerable people?"

"I'm not a doctor. I'm not a psychiatrist or a rocket sci-
entist either. But I know a lot about people in pain."

"Then you know too much," she said quietly.

That contained emotion caused him to make a further offer.
"How about lunch?" He, Evan Thompson, the loner! "Then
we look at furniture, if you like."

"You're being kind, aren't you?" Kindness was there, behind the brooding front. People mattered to him. As they did
to her.

"Kind has nothing to do with it," he said crisply. "I'm
hungry."

"Okay, that would be very nice." She walked towards him
as he rested his powerful body against the doorjamb. "Why
don't you call me Laura?" She gave him a spontaneous smile
that would have had Colin enraged. Her normal smile, or so
she thought. Uncomplicated.

Evan found it captivating. "Then you must call me Evan."
He held out his hand. After a slight hesitation she took it,
her hand getting lost in the size of his.

It was warm and firm, but never hurting.

"There, that wasn't so bad, was it?" he asked, one eye-
brow raised. "You didn't really think I was going to crack
your fingers?" He turned her hand over, examining it. "Delicate, but strong. Are you any good as a pianist?"

The effect of his skin on hers was the most electrifying
thing that had ever happened to her. She couldn't pull away.
It was as though she was held by a naked current. "People
seemed to think so."

"Conservatorium trained?"

"Wh-a-t?" It was so hard to concentrate when every nerve
seemed to be jumping.

He released her hand. "I asked if you were Conservatorium
trained?"

"I graduated. I'd begun studying for my Doctorate of
Music." She managed to speak calmly.

"So what happened?"

"Life."

"An unhappy love affair?" Something had overwhelmed her.

"Desperately unhappy," she admitted. "But that's all you're getting out of me."

"There are worse things than unhappy love affairs," he said.

CHAPTER THREE

IT WAS market day in the town. A day to be enjoyed. Street stalls sold their produce: fruit and vegetables, all sorts of pickles, home-made pies and cakes, the town's excellent cooks vying with one another to come up with some surprises. Stall after stall featured crafts. The town's two cheerful little coffee shops, one hung with red gingham curtains, the other with ruffled pink and white, were crowded.

"Let's get some sandwiches and have a picnic in the park?" Evan suggested. "Would you like that?" He glanced down at her as she stood at his shoulder. No, not his shoulder. A way down from there. More like his heart. Hell, if he wanted to he could pick her up and put her in his pocket.

"Why not?" She smiled at him as if she were treasuring every moment. "Koomera Crossing is such a pretty place. I didn't expect it to be so peaceful and picturesque. The pure air! It's on the edge of the desert, yet lovely warm aromatic breezes are spiraling around us. It's like a thawing of the heart."

"Your heart needs thawing?" he asked, dipping his dark head to her.

"Well, I'm relaxed and comfortable here." she said, looking towards the park, where small children were playing with the balloons they'd been given at the road stalls. "The bauhinia trees are lovely. They'll protect us from the sun while we eat."

"So shall I be mother?" Humour lit his fine eyes. "We don't want to give people too much to talk about." A trained observer, he already knew tongues had been set wagging at their appearance together.

"You know the town better than I do," she conceded, happy when the passing townsfolk nodded to her and Evan in their friendly Outback fashion. "Besides, I might get you something you don't like."

"Would that matter?"

She was conscious of his penetrating glance on her. "Some people are very hard to please," she said by way of explanation.

"Like the boyfriend?" After years of dodging bullets and destruction she seemed too young, too innocent, too unseasoned, to survive.

"We'll have to agree not to talk about him."

"Right. You stay here and soak up the healing sunlight. I'll get the sandwiches and some coffee. Black or white?"

She considered sweetly. "Cappuccino, if they have it."

"Look, you can have a cappuccino, a latte, a mini-cino, a Vienna, a short black, a long black—"

"Thank you. I get the message." She smiled. It was the most incredible thing to be at peace with a man. For all his height and breadth of shoulder, the dark smoulder, he was surprisingly easy to warm to.

"Won't be long." He strode away, glimpsing the town sticky beak, Ruby Hall, peeking through the window of the general store.

He lifted a sardonic hand to wave, but instead of waving back she unsuctioned her nose from the glass.

Dr Sarah Dempsey had come a long way from when she was a girl helping her widowed mother run the store, he thought. After Sarah had left town, Ruby assisted Muriel part-time, inundating everyone who went into the store—which was just about the whole town—with suggestive little questions designed to translate in to hot gossip.

Ruby Hall, nosy parker, really should be stopped, he thought—not for the first time. What she didn't know she made up.

He had attended Mrs Dempsey's funeral—as had most of the town—and shortly after that Sarah had taken over at the hospital from its long-time resident Dr Joe Randall, who had died of cancer at Wunnamurra homestead, stronghold of the

McQueen pioneering family, one of the most powerful landed families in the country.

Now Sarah was shortly to marry Kyall, the heir, as good a man as any woman was likely to get. If his new neighbour had Sarah Dempsey for a friend she had made the right connection.

They sat in rustic wooden chairs beside a bench in the shade of flowering orchid trees and a grove of ancient white gums. White gums flanked the curving banks of the creek, the iridescent green water eddying around small boulders that dotted the stream.

"The stream is the colour of your eyes," he pointed out casually. "A sparkling green."

What a voice he had! Deep, warm, sexy, with that interesting little cutting edge. He even had a slight foreign accent, or was she imagining it?

"It's lovely here," she said happily, incredibly comforted by his presence and the fête-like atmosphere of the town centre. "And to top it off these sandwiches are delicious. Fresh bread, lovely thick ham, just enough lettuce, wholegrain mustard. Perfect." With a total stranger she felt safe.

"Don't forget your cappuccino. It's not terribly good, I'm afraid. I can do better." He reached out a long arm to position it nearer her. "And there's a couple of little cakes."

"One each?"

"They're for you. You seem a tad underweight."

"No doubt because—" She stopped abruptly. She was being seduced by sun and water, the sweetly melancholy song of the magpies, the joyous shrieks of children, and most of all by this big, mesmerizing man who seemed familiar in the deep recesses of her mind.

"You weren't having lots of fun?" He followed up with a question.

"No." She felt a momentary chill as the past brushed up against her.

"What do you intend to do with yourself while you're here?" he asked, his tone brisk.

"Do with myself?" Her voice was startled. "As a matter of fact I haven't thought that far. It's enough to be here."

"You've got yourself in a state if you had to disappear." Her eyelashes quivered. "A breathing space. No more."

"I see." He exuded disbelief.

"Sarah has been marvellous to me. I've been staying with her until I find a place."

"What? In the haunted house? Lucky old you!" His laugh rumbled deep in his chest.

"I'd only been in town ten seconds before I heard about it. But ghosts don't frighten me as much as real people."

He spun his head to stare at her, the dappled shade high-lighting his broad, darkly tanned, handsome face. All he needed was a gold earring and he'd be perfect as a swash-buckling pirate. "Let's get this straight. Your boyfriend was frightening you?"

It was evident he'd never considered for a moment she was married. Did she look so young and inexperienced when she had known such terrible turbulence? "Ye gods! I didn't say that."

"Ye gods?" he gently jeered. "Where did you dig that out? I haven't heard that for years."

"My father used to say it." A sad expression came into her eyes. "He was killed in a car crash when I was eighteen. I adored him."

He nodded, never very far from his own grief. "I miss *my* father terribly. We were very close." He looked away to where a large flock of pink and grey galahs were busily pick-ing over the grass seeds.

"He died?" she said gently.

"Also in a car." He didn't add that he had been murdered by terrorists Evan's own lover had put in motion.

"Are you an only child?" She tried to picture him as a boy. Couldn't. He was so adult. So big. So commanding— even in a short-sleeved blue cotton shirt and jeans, boots on his feet. He made her feel like a doll.

"Like you? Continue the inspection," he invited dryly. "I'm used to being looked over."

She blushed. "You mean by the women of the town?" She heard about this, and understood now she'd meet the high level of feminine interest.

"Women are always looking for a mate," he said, a smile flitting around his handsome mouth.

"But you don't need one." He seemed enormously self-reliant.

He was silent a while. "Of course I need one. But I have to get my life back together before then."

"Your experiences have affected you deeply?"

"Things I don't want to talk about, Laura." Killing fields. Unimaginable brutality.

"So I've learned a lot and yet nothing about you."

"Same here. But you're such a clever thing I'm surprised you can't read my mind."

"I'm doing my best. Do you like music?" she digressed. "Or do you merely pretend? No, you wouldn't pretend, would you?"

"It's never struck me to pretend about such a thing."

"But about other things?"

"We've all got secrets, Laura. Some people have nightmares."

Like me. Laura closed her eyes and knocked a hand to her breast.

"Why did you do that?" He was surprised and rather perturbed by her gesture.

"I don't know. Reflex action. I'm not a very brave person, I'm afraid. Sometimes panic rises up inside me like a flock of birds." As she spoke she looked towards the noisy galahs.

"You're like me. At this point in our lives we need the vastness of the Outback to breathe in. Speaking of music, the highly persuasive Harriet Crompton—that's the town school-teacher—"

"I know Harriet. Sarah introduced us. She's quite a character.'"

"She is." His eyes glittered with amusement. "Dear Harriet drafted me into the town orchestra. I play cello in the string quartet as well."

"Do you really?" She turned in her chair to stare at him.

"Why the arched brows, miss?"

"I thought you looked a little like Beethoven," she teased. "No, seriously, I look on your playing with the orchestra as wonderful. It's just that you seem a very physical man—as in action. It wouldn't surprise me in the least to find out you'd been a commando in your other life."

He grunted wryly. "I can't believe the number of guesses you've had. I told you I'm a wood worker. I'll make you something, if you like. A chair. A table. A jewellery box. Did you bring your diamonds, emeralds and pearls? I bet you've got them."

"Why ever would you say that?" Her voice shook slightly.

"Whatever you've been, Laura, you weren't broke."

She let her long hair slide forward to hide her profile. "It's really weird, the way we're talking so freely, don't you think? We only met an hour or so ago."

"Don't let that bother you. The truth is people have always come to me with their troubles."

"I'm not telling you mine."

"Not even the first chapter? Clearly you don't know how to choose boyfriends. Why in hell are you running anyway? Won't he take no for an answer?"

"Be nice. Get off the subject," she begged.

"Okay. Providing we can continue at another time. You're not dieting, are you?"

"Good grief, no. Can't you see? I ate the sandwiches."

"Then eat the cakes. They cost good money and I've no intention of throwing them away."

"All right, then." She picked up one of the little home-made cup cakes. "Have you finally found your role?" She glanced mischievously at him out of the side of her green eyes.

"As in big brother?" he asked sarcastically. Far better to treat her that way. "I feel almost geriatric beside you." She carried with her the innocence and freshness of spring.

"At thirty-seven, thirty-eight?"

"I stopped being young long ago," he said too bluntly.

"Now, when you're finished I think we ought to hit the Trading Post. They sell new furniture as well as old." He raised a quizzical brow. "How do you intend to pay for it all?"

"Why?" She raised an anxious face, always worried about endangering herself, bringing Colin after her.

"So I can be sure the name on your credit card matches the name you told me. Laura Graham."

"I can pay in cash."

"Cash?" His deep voice slid dismally. "Surely you're not carrying around lots of cash?"

"Hey, cash will do."

"Don't you have credit cards? It's illegal for banks to give away private information."

"Surely people can find out anything if they want to?"

He shook his head, staring into her face, past and beyond it. "Why don't you tell me all about it on the way home?"

"No thank you, big brother," she joked. "You mustn't worry about me."

"On the contrary, I might have to." He disposed tidily of the café's take-away boxes and paper cups. "If for no other reason than you're going to be my next-door neighbour."

"There's something comforting in that," she said, feeling safer than she had at any time since she'd lost another big, strong man radiating kindness and authority. Her father.

Picking out furniture proved to be the greatest fun. They wandered through the store, which was divided into two sections—Used and New Furniture—debating what would go where. Evan must have called in on the Lawsons, the owners of the cottage a few times, she reasoned, because he had an exact knowledge of the layout and dimensions of the various rooms.

"Yah goin' house-huntin', little lady?" The salesman, a lanky laconic middle-aged man, followed them around, wedging himself between Laura and every piece of furniture she particularly wanted to see.

"I've found it." She smiled pleasantly.

"The young lady will be renting the Lawsons' cottage for

a while,'' Evan intervened. ''Don't worry about showing us around, Zack. We'll wander about, then get back to you when we find what we like.''

''Sure thing, Evan,'' Zack said cheerily. ''Listen, I got folks wanting those carved armchairs you've been makin'. They were real successful. You sure are a gifted guy, what with playin' the cello and all. Me wife keeps tellin' me it's so romantic; I think I'll go back to playin' my ukelele. Might fill in a few evening's. Reckon I could sell anything you cared to make. We've never had a cabinet maker anythin' like you,'' he added fervently. ''Folks around here just love yah designs. Reckon yah could put the price up easily without goin' over the top. Folks would be willin' to pay.''

''I'll think about it, Zack. And thanks for the nice compliments.''

''We're partners, ain't we? You make. I sell. Tell yah somethin' else. Folks love yah boxes. Sold the last one to Tessy Matthews for her weddin' chest.''

''That's great! Had I known it was for her wedding chest she could have had it for nothing.''

''Folks don't treasure what they get for nuthin','' Zack maintained.

''You're a smart, smart man, Zack.'' Evan laughed, steering Laura through the archway that led to the secondhand section.

''You get along with him okay?''

''Why not? I've never had any trouble getting along with people. Even very difficult people.'' He remembered the number of men holding guns he had interviewed. Some genuine patriots. Others a bunch of fruitcakes.

''Yet you've earned the reputation of being something of a loner.''

''Is that so?''

She nodded. ''Difficult to sustain when the young women of the town are on a crusade to draw you out?''

''Who told you that, precisely, Laura?''

''I've seen it with my own eyes.'' Indeed, she had noted the curiosity and interest as they moved amid the smiling sea

of faces. probably they were already an item of hot gossip in
the coffee shops, with a dazzle of gazes through the colonial
windows. ''Harriet mentioned it as well, if I'm not telling
tales.''

''Harriet's a throwback to everyone's slightly astringent
favourite aunt.'' Evan grinned. ''So, Harriet told you there
are women anxious to enjoy my company?''

''*I* like being with you,'' she pointed out, as though that
were entirely reasonable. ''You're bracing and kindly.''

''Hell, I'm not your goddamn grandfather,'' he retorted.
''You seem to prize kindliness in a man above all else.''

''Every woman wants a man who will be kind to her and
her children,'' Laura answered, very seriously indeed.

''And you're worried that your boyfriend isn't a great
choice for life?''

''Correct,'' There was pain and sorrow in it.

''But you miss him already?''

''I'd like to ask you a few questions, Mr Thompson,'' she
retaliated. ''If you answer truthfully my lips are sealed. Are
you married?''

''Never. Not once.'' He looked directly at her.

''How come?''

''For a lot of years of my life I never knew where I was
going to wake up.''

''What does that mean, exactly?'' She'd already sensed he
was a man of adventure.

''On the move, Laura. I've travelled the world.''

''As a wood worker?'' she queried dubiously.

''When I could find the time.''

''Don't you miss it?''

''Miss what?'' He bent to examine a small desk. A few
scars. Nothing that couldn't be fixed.

''Whatever you did. I'm not so totally inexperienced I
can't see you were personally acquainted with danger.''

''So much for my tight cover.'' he mock-growled.

''You won't always live here, will you?'' she persisted,
accepting the powerful natural attraction of him.

''No more than you. In fact I marvel at the fact you found

your way out here. This is truly the Outback, the Never Never, the Back of Beyond.''

"I love it already,'' Laura said, her lovely face dreamy. "The peace, the freedom, the vastness. I've decided I'm going to walk every inch of the Simpson Desert,'' she joked. "Maybe I'll take a pack of camels, like that wonderful woman author. I can't remember her name at the moment, but I was fascinated by her book.''

"Robyn Davidson. The name of her book was *Tracks*. It's an account of her 1700-mile journey across Australia with camels. It won her an award.''

"You're very knowledgable.'' She looked at a coffee table, thinking about where it might go.

"Yes,'' he agreed.

"You're a writer? You're a famous author?''

His brilliant gaze told her she was way off beam. "Let's get this whole thing cleared up. I'm a wood worker.''

She was afraid she had overstepped the mark. "I'm sorry. I don't mean to pry, Evan. I was just having—fun.''

"Hey!'' He watched her face, saw it lose colour. That really bothered him. "I'm sorry too if I sounded a bit stern. Who hurt you, Laura?'' he questioned, looking like a man who would listen. "If I don't ask I'll never know.''

Her eyes clouded. "Why do you want to know?''

"There's something very endearing about you,'' he said with simple truth. "Witness the way you've cajoled reclusive me to take you out for coffee and sandwiches. Just between the two of us I want to know enough to be on the look-out for your boyfriend, should he decide to try to track you down. Do you think he will?''

Her whole body tensed. "No, no. Everything's okay.''

"Of course. That's why you just trembled. I promise you I'll keep an eye out, and you don't have to put me on the payroll. Maybe you can invite me in for dinner some time. Can you cook?''

She smiled. Shook her head. "I thought I could. Now I'm not so sure.''

"Your self-esteem has taken a battering.''

"Why do you say that."

"It couldn't be clearer if it were front page news on today's *Courier Mail*."

"There you go again." She paused in her inspection of a sofa to look across at him. "You're a reporter. An overseas correspondent. There's something else in your background, I think."

"Please tell me," he invited, deliberately using a casual tone. He continued down the aisle, thinking she was way too perceptive.

"This might be a bad time for it as you're helping me choose my furniture."

"Fire away." He touched his fingers to the surface of a smallish circular table. Good red cedar. "I won't hold it against you."

"All right." A curious thrill raced down Laura's spine. "I know we only met today. And I've never seen you before in my life. Yet the more I look at you the more I'm convinced I know your face from somewhere. Have you ever worn a beard?"

"Good grief, Laura." He rolled out a leather armchair on castors.

"Tell the truth."

"Every man has a beard from time to time, even if it's only the weekend growth."

"I mean a full beard and moustache."

"My dear, that would take years," he drawled.

"All right. It's just that I keep seeing you with a beard. Very impressive. Very formidable. As though no one could hide from you. The cover of a book, maybe?"

He exchanged a droll look with her. "You're not even warm." Which was far from the truth. He *had* put out a book on his trip to Antarctica—but the photograph had been on the back cover, beard and all. "But I'll guarantee to give progress reports."

"Just a woman's curiosity." She settled in the rich burgundy armchair he had rolled out for her attention.

"And here I was thinking you a mere babe," he gently mocked.

"I know." It was true she didn't carry her scars on her face, otherwise she would look awful.

He couldn't help smiling at the picture she made, curled up in the oversized but very comfortable chair.

"But very bright. When you're older and more sure of yourself you'll be positively dangerous." He turned to look around him. "We've walked all the aisles. What do you think?"

"The armchair, definitely," she decided. "It's very cosy. I liked the circular table you were looking at. Good wood. Is it red cedar?"

"It is. It'll come up nicely."

"You mean you're going to work on it?" she asked, sliding her long hair back behind her ear.

"When I have the time. What else?"

"The most expensive thing will be the new bedroom suite," she said. "We can use the cedar table for when I invite you in. I'm not fussed on the chairs. They're too—functional. Clean lines." Her smile was strained.

"You and the boyfriend got to discussing furnishings?" Instantly he picked up on her wavelength.

"How do you know I'm not married?" She looked straight at him, loving his attention and the dazzling complexity of it, but somehow hoping he would guess her secret.

"I don't know," he replied, studying her with his brilliant dark eyes. "You'd say, wouldn't you? Then again I can't remember when I last met a young woman who somehow struck me as being such an innocent abroad."

"I'm not. Maybe I'm playing at a character."

He didn't speak for a few moments, considering what she'd just said. "I don't think so. I think you're a young woman who's been cherished all your life and now you find yourself in a situation you can't handle. Yet you're someone who wants desperately to stand on your own two feet. You're even prepared to take a risk to do it. Is the boyfriend someone who wants to dominate you?"

"Very much so." She couldn't keep the quiver out of her voice.

"Then it's clear you can't be happy together. Probably that's why you're comfortable with me. You are, aren't you?"

She flushed. "Yes."

He nodded. "You're drawn to older men. No doubt because you deeply loved your father."

"Yes, again. Isn't it a mercy that as well as being comfortable—which you're not, strictly—you're charming, obliging, with a good sense of humour, and investigative enough to be interesting? Shall I go on? You shouldn't be worried I'll take advantage of your kindness. I half hope we'll be friends?"

"Why half hope?" He lifted a quizzical brow.

"I can't expect more."

"You can as far as I'm concerned. The decision has been made. I'm big brother. You're Laura next door. We're well on our way towards becoming good friends. To put the whole thing simply, we've bonded. Both of us are living defensively and so forth. As for chairs—I have two at home that will do you nicely."

"Did you make them?" She looked up at him with open delight.

"I did."

"Then I'm honoured. I heard you don't charge a lot either."

"Laura they're a house-warming present," he said gently.

"Oh I can't—" she started, broke off, overwhelmed by his kindness and generosity.

"Yes, you can. Now, there are a few other things you can have sent. That coffee table, for one. Cash cover it?" he asked in a laconic voice.

"It does, and I like it."

"Those few little nicks can be ironed out. No problem at all to bring it back to its former glory. What about that coat-stand for the hall? I don't think it will crowd it. I expect you'll wear a lot of hats. You'll need them to protect your skin. You won't be needing a raincoat, however. I can't even remember when it last rained. When do you think you will move in?''

A smile curved her lips. "If it can be organised, why not tomorrow?''

"I'm sure it can. I'll be on hand to help out.''

"Why are you being so nice?" All at once her heart was beating fast. All wrong, in the circumstances.

"You're a woman on your own, aren't you?" he said reasonably. "I'm the kind of man who likes to lend a hand.''

"Then I'm very grateful.''

"Besides, I've had a good time.'' He looked at her and gave that white melting smile that sat so piquantly with his dark, brooding good looks. "I was getting terribly dull. Terribly set in my ways.''

"I wonder how long it will be before you're ever that.''

"Laura Graham, you scare me.'' Before he could help himself he had touched her cheek lightly with his finger. It had the velvety texture of a magnolia.

For a moment they stared into one another's eyes. Laura felt oddly as if the air might explode.

"Well, come on," he said, making a brisk return to the role of big brother. "We really should visit the general store. You'll be needing a few pots and pans, though you don't look like you eat a whole lot.''

"Don't go thinking I have eating problems," she chided him.

"So why the feather weight?''

He spoke lightly, but she couldn't help herself going tense. "I don't know really. It's not easy to eat sometimes.''

"When you're unhappy and you're sleeping badly?" His dark eyes rested on her for a second.

"I'm going to deal with it.''

"Good girl," he said quietly.

Together they began to walk back along the aisle. Laura felt so drawn to him, but she had no doubts that before he'd come to Koomera Crossing he'd been someone very differ-

ent. He'd lived a high-powered life, running on adrenaline.
Perhaps even in personal danger.

Who was he? Unless he told her she could speculate for
ever and never know. As for him she realized he saw an
image of a vulnerable little rich girl on the run from some
very smart, demanding boyfriend in her set. She wondered
what he would think if she told him about Colin and the
wreck of a marriage. He would be kind but he might secretly
despise her for failing to stand up to the enemy.

She told Sarah all about her day over the evening meal. Laura
had prepared cashew nut and ginger chicken, served with
Chinese noodles and a side dish of crisp green broccoli flo-
rets.

"Mmm, this is great! I'm really going to miss you,
Laura." Sarah looked up from her plate to smile. "It's lovely
having a meal waiting for me when I get home from the
hospital, and you're such a good cook. You and Harriet ought
to get together. She's thinking of retiring from schoolteaching
and starting up a restaurant."

"Here in the town?" Laura was intrigued.

"Kyall convinced her we could do with a good restaurant.
All we have are the two coffee shops. They only sell snacks.
Harriet is a marvellous and adventurous chef. She loves everything to do with food. She's collected stacks of recipes on
her travels. Thailand. India. She goes for exotica. I believe
she could make quite a success of it."

"How exciting for her." Laura nodded her agreement
quickly. "One career closes. Another opens."

"And what are you going to do with yourself while you're
here?" Sarah looked up to pin Laura's green gaze.

"Evan asked me exactly the same thing."

"So what did you tell him?"

"That I haven't thought that far. I didn't tell him I was
married. Did I make a mistake, Sarah? I couldn't, for some
reason. He's so intuitive he immediately cottoned onto the
fact I was on the run. But he surmised a boyfriend."

Sarah studied Laura's down-bent face. "You do have a certain look of—"

"Innocent at large?" Laura asked dismally. "I must correct that."

"No one would know from looking at you the awful experiences you've been through. It's the lovely gentle look, the white skin. I'm not surprised Evan jumped to the conclusion you're unmarried. Evidently you brought out the protective streak in him."

"I must have." Laura blushed. "From what I'd gathered I expected someone quite aloof, or at least with considerable reserve."

"He can be like that," Sarah conceded thoughtfully. "He's certainly disappointed a lot of women around here. They're fascinated with his aura. He doesn't smile often, which is a pity because—"

"When he does it's like the sun coming out," Laura interjected. "He has a beautiful smile."

Sarah dimpled. "I'm so glad you got on well together. I didn't think you'd take the cottage, actually. It's so small. But I'm sure you can make it comfortable. It's good to know Evan Thompson will be right next door. I wouldn't care to tackle him if I were in the wrong. There's one man who knows how to take care of himself."

"I don't think that's his real name, do you?"

Sarah tipped her head to the side. "A great deal of speculation goes on about Evan. Even Kyall is thoroughly intrigued. The two of them get on well. Obviously Evan's not what he purports to be—a wood worker. Though I believe his pieces are simply beautiful. I intend to follow that up."

"He's promised me two chairs."

"Gracious, it could be the start of a collection," Sarah teased. "Evan must have treated you very nicely. You're looking so much more relaxed."

"I'm starting to feel it." Laura spoke softly, gratefully.

"That's good. When you feel strong enough you'll have to address the problem of Colin, though I know it won't be easy."

"No. A year of his cruelty has left me with many self-doubts and fear."

Sarah reached out and gripped her hand. "You have friends. There are ways of protecting you. Now there's Evan. A man like Colin would have to be very brave to mess around with him."

"What if he finds out I have a violent husband?"

Sarah studied Laura's face, knowing full well the terrible psychological damage victims of abuse suffered. "The right moment will come to alert him."

"Yes." Laura's answer was hopeful. "I suspect Colin is already looking for me. Probably he thinks I'm hiding out somewhere in New Zealand. He'll have contacted my mother to see if she knows where I am."

"And does she?" Sarah hoped not, for both women's sake.

"No." Laura shook her gleaming dark head. "It will be a lot better for Mum if she doesn't know. I wrote her a long letter before I left, trying to explain how unhappy I was. I didn't paint Colin as the villain he is. I'm too ashamed."

"You did nothing wrong, Laura," Sarah consoled her, aware this was a common reaction.

Laura looked away. "I should have made a run for freedom long before this. I took a year of fear, degradation and punishment. You wouldn't have taken it, Sarah. You have such confidence and purpose about you."

Sarah's expression changed. "I'm not the strong, problem-confronting woman you think I am, Laura. I'm no more invincible than you. I find being a doctor deeply satisfying, but I've made lots of mistakes in my emotional life. I've lived with unresolved issues for far too long. I've always made the excuse that I've been uncertain of the outcome if I tackled them. I'm still learning about my own self. I don't suppose we ever stop."

Laura looked across the table. Saw a beautiful blonde woman with velvety dark eyes. There was nothing weak or ineffectual about Sarah Dempsey. She looked strong. In control of her life. Laura deeply envied her. "You wouldn't allow a man to physically and sexually abuse you, Sarah. You have an inner self-assurance I don't have.''

''You're so young, Laura. Even now.'' Sarah endeavoured to comfort her. ''Abusers—men like Colin—pick their mark. They're drawn to gentle, sensitive women and they like to get them young. Had you been a few years older he mightn't have found it quite so easy, but circumstances played right into his hands. At that time you needed support—not just emotional. You'd lost your father, your mother had remarried and gone away, and then your husband cut you off from your friends. He did enormous damage. What a cruel man he must be. All those times we met at functions and I never suspected for a minute he could possibly be violent with you. He behaved as though he adored you while behind the scenes he made you suffer.'' Sarah shook her head in disbelief.

''Even my mother was fooled. I'm sure she doesn't know what to think even now. Colin will have told her such lies. Colin the ruthless manipulator. He's so convincing. You've seen that. He'll make my mother think I have problems handling the role of wife to a very successful cardiologist. A man who saves lives. Colin always used to sneer at me. Say I'd been over-protected. Wrapped in cotton wool. The classic Daddy's Little Girl, as he said. I loved both my parents. Losing my father has only made me love him more.''

''Of course, Laura. Coming from such a happy, stable home you were ill-prepared to take on Colin's aberrant behaviour. But I too know all about powerlessness and humiliation. I'll tell you about it some time. Meanwhile, you've got enough on your plate.''

CHAPTER FOUR

IT WAS mid-morning when the furniture van arrived.

"Careful, Snowy!" Zack warned his young offsider as they tried to manoeuvre a sofa through the small doorway.

It was clear Snowy wasn't listening, or he had no aptitude for these activities.

"Steady on, boy!" Zack shouted the caution. "Miss Laura here ain't gunna be happy if you knock a chunk out of the front door."

"Won't go in, Zack. The bloody doorway's too narrow," Snowy offered miserably.

"Language, son. No need to swear." Zack cast an embarrassed glance at Laura as though she had never heard a single swear-word in her life.

"Sorry, miss." Snowy made a distraught movement of his ash-blond head.

"Put it down for a minute," Zack said crossly, his temper still simmering from yesterday. Snowy was always breaking something—forcing it. He still had a lump on his head the size of a plum from yesterday's mishap with a wardrobe—but Snowy was the wife's nephew. A more than usually stubborn boy, with not all the cards in the pack. Took after his dad's side of the family, of course…

"Having problems?" Evan Thompson appeared on the open verandah of the colonial next door, looking the very picture of the legendary alpha man.

"You could say that!" Zack replied with sarcasm.

"Give me a minute; I'll be there."

"Thanks, mate!" Zack called back more cheerfully. A smart guy like Evan would make this manoeuvre the easiest thing imaginable.

Evan waved a response then went back to the phone, finishing off his progress report to the agent who was eager to market his book.

Moments later he pushed the little picket gate of the cottage. It needed to be open. Who had closed it? Laura was standing on the tiny porch wearing a little ruffled yellow sundress that made a pool of light. Her long silky hair was drawn back into a knot, exposing her pretty ears, delicate bone structure and the long lovely line of her throat.

"Good morning!" A day and already he was far too involved with this young woman. Certainly his eyes had fallen in love with her beauty. The fatal flaw in him: his susceptibility to beauty.

"Good morning, Evan," she responded, so happily it touched his iron-clad heart. "It's so nice of you to come."

"I'd have been here earlier, only I had to field a few calls. So what's the problem, Zack?"

Zack gave him a frustrated look. "Snowy here don't seem capable of negotiating the front door."

"Yah'd better believe it!" said Snowy, treading backwards and bumping into the planter's chair he had already placed on the porch.

"I'd be real grateful if yah could take his end, Evan." Zack snorted his disgust.

"No problem." Evan had solved it on sight.

"Not my idea to be a removalist," Snowy defended himself, relinquishing his end without argument. "I told Mum but she called me a lazy bum. That's exactly what she said, 'Snowy, you're a lazy bum.'"

Evan laughed. "And you're saying that's not the case?"

"I wish she'd listen." Snowy's voice dropped dolefully as he watched the two men make short work of getting the sofa through the narrow doorway.

"Make yahself useful, Snowy." Zack took a couple of beats to yell at him. "Go get the little stuff."

"I'll help you, Snowy," Laura said, anxious to be useful herself, and sorry for the unfortunate young man.

"That's okay, miss." Snowy lost his gloomy look, going

a bright pink under his freckled tan. "I don't want you doin'
nuthin'. Besides, Zack is takin' yah money."

"Well, well, you made quite a conquest with Snowy," Evan
observed some thirty minutes later as the furniture van pulled
away. "He's got a giant crush on you already."

"I think I believe you!" Laura paused in her rearranging
to smile. "He doesn't seem at all suited to help Zack out in
the business."

"From what Zack told me he's been responsible for some
major damage," Evan answered dryly. "As a removalist
Snowy seems a complete incompetent. I wonder if he could
find work on one of the outlying stations. From all accounts
he's very good around horses. He told me he loves to be
outdoors. I might have a word with Mitch Claydon. The
Claydons—you'll be meeting them—own Marjimba cattle
station. The McQueens have always stuck to sheep—
Australia produces the world's finest wool—but Wunnamurra
is only a small part of their business interests these days.
They're big. I can tell you that. You've heard about the
McQueens from Sarah?"

"Not a lot." Laura settled a few cushions on the sofa,
looked around for his approving nod. "Sarah has been too
busy listening to me. I've met Kyall twice, when he's called
in to the house. What a splendid couple they make! Very
obviously he's deeply in love with Sarah, and she with him.
But a few odd comments around the place have made me
wonder if there's some secret family business. Sarah keeps
hinting I might hear something soon."

"Well, then…" He shrugged, pushing a small bookcase
against the wall. "It's no secret Sarah doesn't get on with
Kyall's grandmother, Ruth McQueen."

"I gathered that. She's a formidable lady?"

"That doesn't say it." His handsome mouth compressed.
Ruth McQueen, matriarch of that powerful family had all but
repelled him on their few encounters. In her seventies and
still a striking-looking woman; it was more to do with her

aura. He'd met people like Ruth McQueen in his other life. Ruthless people. People one didn't cross with impunity.

"But Sarah will be part of the family?" Laura turned as she spoke, making a forlorn little gesture with her hands.

"Yes," he agreed—like Laura, thinking of its implications. He let his eyes linger on her. He had to realize he was becoming too protective of her on some deep elemental level. Maybe it was her size. He towered over her. Maybe it was her inherent sensitivity, her vulnerability?

"Sarah did tell you she and Kyall have been bonded since childhood? Apparently it's been quite a love story. Everyone in town knows about it. I expect you do too."

"We haven't really caught up. Sarah's determined to help me."

"Do what?"

"Find my feet, I suppose." She sank onto the deep yellow sofa, colourful crushed velvet cushions piled all around her. "Sarah is such a strong person. I'm very wobbly compared to her."

He shifted the coffee table a fraction, then took the armchair opposite her. His back was to the sunshine that streamed into the room. It danced around her in golden beams. "We've all got wobbly areas, Laura. I think Sarah, for all her inner strength, carries a few burdens. She'll have them for some time while Ruth McQueen is around."

"But in the end the most tremendous thing is she'll have Kyall's love and support. One only has to see them together to know their marriage will work."

"And you're very fearful yours won't?"

"What do you mean?" Her heart suddenly pounded, though she did her best to hide her agitation.

"I thought that was clear," he answered mildly, thoroughly aware of the change in her. "For whatever reasons you're fleeing your own relationship. Obviously you don't trust your boyfriend enough to marry him. He mustn't provide you with a sense of security. Or you don't love him enough. Do you?" The look he aimed at her was very direct.

Flustered, she looked away. "I thought I did. Once. He put so much into our courtship. Showered me with gifts."

My God, wouldn't that be easy? Showering this beautiful creature with gifts. "Well, he wasn't getting a bad bargain," he gently mocked.

"A beautiful, gifted wife in the making."

"He didn't make me feel that."

"So why didn't you confront him with it?" He frowned. "Why did you continue the relationship at all?"

She clasped her ringless hands together. "I can't find the answers."

"You're very young, Laura. You're only in the process of becoming the woman you're going to be. Why do you think people make so many mistakes when they're young? Living is all about the getting of wisdom."

She took a quiet breath, nodded. "At least I'm beginning to see more clearly. I lost the protection of my father," she added poignantly

"Protection?" His head went up and a glitter invaded his dark eyes.

"I haven't been terribly clever with my life up to date, Evan. You've surmised that, I desperately needed good advice, but as it happened there was a lack of it. I'd like to be stronger, more able to defend myself, but it won't happen overnight. I need time to change my world and my position in it. Most of my friends always were far more sophisticated than I. My friend Ellie used to have a little running joke about me being the Sleeping Beauty."

"Evidently you haven't found your prince?"

"Are there princes in this world?" All at once she knew there were. The woman this man loved would find a safe haven, a powerful benign presence. Solidity.

"My answer is yes, Laura. You told me you adored your father. Weren't your parents happy?"

"Wonderfully happy," she sighed. "My father was the kindest man in the world. He was marvellous."

"Why can't you talk to your mother?"

"She lives in New Zealand. She married a sheep farmer a

few years after we lost Dad. She had one happy marriage. She wanted another. My mother can't live without a man.''

''Wouldn't most women want to be in a relationship?''

''Better to be on one's own than unhappy.''

''So why endure a relationship that's not working? What's the worst thing about this boyfriend of yours? I don't hear his name.''

''I can't talk about him yet, Evan.'' Even Colin's name made her feel in insecure.

''Okay. But you've confided in Sarah? You need someone to talk to?''

''Sarah is another woman and she's very understanding. I consider myself very lucky to have her for a friend.''

''How long have you known her?''

She'd have liked to say for ages, but she had to tell the truth. ''A year, on and off.''

''And here I was thinking you'd known one another for ever.''

''Getting to know someone in a day isn't all that impossible.'' She knew she held his dark gaze longer than she should. ''You think people are going to be one thing and they turn out to be quite another.''

''I assume you're referring to me?''

She couldn't say she was referring to her Jekyll and Hyde husband. She evaded the answer. ''How did you get to be as tough as you are?'' She couldn't find the precise word, but there was nothing remotely soft about him. He was very much the man. The man of steel.

''Tough?'' He sounded unconvinced.

''You carry that image. I don't mean tough as in rough.'' She coloured a little. ''Certainly not. I mean able to meet challenges head-on. To be a resilient, functioning, strong individual who can handle whatever life throws at you.''

He laughed without humour, remembering how it was. ''Laura, it was a big struggle. I have my moments of inner devastation.''

''But you carry on?'' She couldn't leave this question of personal inner strength alone. She carried so much self-disgust at the punishment she had taken during her short marriage.

He saw her eyes, beautiful, haunted. "Why are you so unhappy? It can't be simply a fear of plunging into marriage with the wrong person?"

She pulled a sapphire blue cushion onto her lap. "Have you ever been in love, or felt or thought you were in love?"

His mouth quirked. "I figure at thirty-eight I must have been."

"And the woman I resemble?"

The sombre expression was back in place. "You don't resemble her at all. A figure-type—petite and slender. The way you wear your hair." He wanted to reach over and pull her hair out of its loose knot, watch its silken slide around her romantic face.

"You were in love with her?"

"Questions, questions!"

"If you can ask them so can I."

"I was in love with the woman I thought she was. She was never that person," he said, his eyes disturbingly dark.

"I'm sorry." She was afraid that woman had badly hurt him. "So, has it taken a long time for you to become involved with anyone else?"

His deep attractive voice was full of amusement. "I certainly don't intend becoming involved with you, miss."

"I know that." Yet something in his eyes made her head whirl. "I'm not planning any involvements for a very long time. Maybe never. We're two people who escaped out here to breathe."

"Exactly." His tone was calm.

"It's extraordinary the way I feel free to talk to you." By doing so she felt she was helping herself.

"What's your boyfriend's profession?" he surprised her by asking.

"He's a doctor." The words were uttered; too late to take them back.

"Am I hearing correctly? A doctor?" He frowned. "I would have thought a doctor would be an understanding person. Caring for people is what their calling is all about. For most of them it's very important. I've known some heroic doctors in my time.''

They weren't about inflicting cruelty and pain, Laura thought.

In front of his eyes her whole demeanour altered. ''Do you doubt your ability to carry off the role of doctor's wife?''

She gave a restless little shake of her head. ''It could be I'm not fit to be a wife at all.''

''Stop putting yourself down. You shouldn't do it.''

''Lots of things I shouldn't be doing, Evan.'' She sighed and tried to smile. ''Like sitting here with you when we should be up working.''

''I can take care of the work.'' He stood up, filling the small parlour with his sheer presence. ''I can tell you one thing, Laura. You don't need anyone in your life who remorselessly drains off all your self-confidence.''

''I'll have to start thinking like you. I might take up judo or karate.''

''Power, kiddo? Is that what you're hoping to achieve?'' He laughed, looking down at her ethereal frame.

''If I were stronger I might be more in control,'' she said, very seriously. ''I think my image is much too soft and dreamy. It speaks of weakness.''

''Nonsense! I'd stick to your image, if I were you. It's perfectly beautiful. Surely you couldn't fail to know that?''

''Sarah is beautiful, but one senses immediately she's strong. I so admire her.''

''Laura, my dear, you are simply too hard on yourself. Possibly you've allowed yourself to be brainwashed. Is the boyfriend a fitness freak?''

She grimaced a little. ''Yes, but he doesn't have a black belt.'' Otherwise he might have killed me.

''I do,'' he said casually. ''I was always interested in the martial arts. I like the discipline, austerity, mastering difficult techniques and working on the concentration that's needed. Overall it's a great feeling of achievement. In my early days one of my workout partners was a young girl. I was terrified

I would hurt her. She was tiny. Like you. By the end of the class I had nothing but respect for her. She was a whirlpool of energy. I know I left the class pretty sore.''

''Can you teach me?'' Suddenly she was presented with an idea.

''I'd rather not.'' He didn't want to get too physically close to her for any number of reasons. Number one being his strong sexual attraction to her. He couldn't do a damned thing about it. Little Miss Graham was way off-limits.

''That's the first mean thing you've said.''

''Laura, I could scarcely bear to hurt you,'' he groaned. Didn't she know how she looked? So fragile, so graceful in her movements. It was the last thing he wanted but he felt a sharp stab of desire.

''May I remind you of your little sparring partner?''

''She'd long been in training,'' he clipped off. ''You might feel very differently if you were to go flying through the air. Falls can be very painful.''

''Then can you show me a few moves?'' Her fear of Colin had been greatly compounded by his physical superiority. Would he have been so free with his hands had she been able to strike back?

He pressed a hand to his strong jawline. ''I'll think about it. Demons are in your head, Laura,'' he told her ruefully. ''You can vanquish them using mind control.''

''I'd feel better if you could show me a few defensive moves.''

He stared down at her, vaguely astonished. He couldn't handle the thought of hurting her.

''You'd show a younger sister, wouldn't you?'' she challenged, green eyes sparkling. ''Or your favourite female cousin?''

''Let me think about it, Laura,'' he replied.

''I used to study ballet, you know,'' she offered, as if that would help.

''That's a hell of a start.''

''Ballet dancers are very strong and athletic. I was very

good, but I had to stop when I was about fourteen. I didn't have the time with my music.''

Her appearance was even at odds with her piano-playing, though he knew size could be deceptive. The one time they had shaken hands her fingers had been long, delicate, but they had to be strong.

''By the way, its no problem to get you access to the town's grand piano,'' he said, knowing how much a musician needed constant contact with their chosen instrument. ''It was a gift from the McQueen family. No second-rate instrument. A Steinway.''

''Good grief, how generous.'' She stood a foot away, petals of colour in her magnolia cheeks.

''Yes, indeed,'' he agreed dryly. ''Sing out when you're ready. For now, let's tackle the kitchen. I'll help you unpack those boxes.''

''Evan, you've been so kind. I can finish up.''

''I'll get things out of the boxes for you. You won't want them in your way. And I'll get them back to Zack. This is going to be quite pretty, actually.'' He looked about. ''A doll's house for a French doll.''

''Who's going to learn karate!'' She struck a little pose, clean, balletic, extremely beautiful.

''I ask myself, how did I get myself into this?''

''Stop puzzling over it. Maybe it was meant to be. Can you shoot?''

''I hate guns,'' he said harshly.

''Then you're used to them. You know what they can do.''

''Young lady, there is no way I'm going to show you how to handle a rifle. It's against the law.''

''Unless one has a licence. There are a lot of licences out here in the Outback.''

''Laura, what are you getting at?'' She was leading the way to the kitchen but he found himself catching the point of her shoulder, turning her to him.

''I'm pretty sure a lot of women would feel safer if they had a gun.''

"I'm pretty sure a lot of lives could be lost that way as well. You don't need any gun."

"I don't want one. I hate them too."

"Please look me in the eye."

"Yes, Evan." She lifted her head.

"You can't really believe your life's in danger?"

"Of course it isn't. Probably I was trying to shock you."

"Believe me, you have."

"Okay, I'm done." She stared into the brilliant dark depths of his eyes, wishing desperately she had nothing to hide.

"Good." Abruptly he moved, before he made the fatal mistake of taking her into his arms. "Let's get cracking."

He led her into the kitchen where several boxes were stacked. He knew they contained a dinner set, cutlery, pots and pans, electrical goods, a frypan, toaster, kettle, kitchen linen, glasses marked "Fragile".

"Don't lift that one," he said, pointing downwards. "It's too heavy."

"You have to stop looking at me like I'm a piece of porcelain," she said. "Not very complimentary to me."

"But understandable," he said dryly, allowing his eyes to move over her.

"Well, I'm not. You should hear me thunder out Chopin's *Revolutionary Etude*."

He was acutely aware of her slender body resting against the counter so near to him. The whiteness of her skin made her gleaming hair appear almost black. Her green eyes shimmered like jewels. There was no question the boyfriend was madly in love with her. He himself was staggered by the level of intimacy he had achieved with this troubled young woman.

"The spirit, no doubt, Laura. It's an inner power true musicians have."

The sound of his deep voice touched her clear through to her centre. It reverberated like a deep, deep purr, reminding her that the human voice was the greatest instrument of all.

For total strangers they'd had a great deal to say to each

other. Ships that passed in the night? Brief encounters?
Intuitively she understood that behind the complex exterior
was a gallantry a woman could count on. After a year of
brutal punishment it was like a marvellous healing balm.

CHAPTER FIVE

LAURA could feel the vibrancy in Sarah the minute she swept through the door. Sarah looked on top of the world, beautifully strong and womanly. She even moved as if beautiful music was going on in her head. Music she could dance to.

"Gosh, you look happy!" Laura could see Sarah was excited. Colour spread over her high cheekbones. Her dark eyes glittered.

Sarah turned to beam at her. "I'm like a new woman. Full of wonder and delight."

"That's lovely," Laura's voice was gentle. She was moved by such happiness. "How nice of you to find the time to call."

Sarah dropped her shoulder bag onto an empty hook on the hall stand. "I wish I could have come sooner, but so much has been happening. You'll be amazed. I'm still in a state of shock and euphoria."

"So tell me," Laura invited, quickly leading the way into the parlour.

"First I want to see what you've done here." Sarah glanced around with genuine admiration. "You are a home-maker." Laura had accomplished a great deal without obvious expense. She had used a light palette of colours and a mix of furnishings and had managed to make them harmonious. "You've made it very comfortable and attractive, Laura. I'm so pleased for you."

"These are the chairs I told you about. A house-warming gift from Evan. Do you like them?" Laura inclined her head towards the front window, where two light-grained polished wood chairs flanked a small circular table.

"I do, indeed." Sarah moved to take a closer look.

"They add a touch of class, don't you think?"

"As does Evan." Sarah laughed. "He certainly is multi-talented. He's a fine musician too, did he tell you?"

"Cello," Laura confirmed. "His mother taught him when he was a boy. I have an idea she's well known, but he didn't want to be drawn."

"That's Evan." Sarah shrugged, sinking into one of the comfortable armchairs. "How's the friendship progressing?"

"Time will tell." Laura smiled. "He may tire of being a Good Samaritan, but I'm revelling in having him next door. There's nothing he can't fix. Colin used to call in a professional to change the halogen lights. I have to say the ceilings were very high, but I can't imagine Evan doing any such thing."

"No." Sarah grinned. "He certainly exudes competence. There's a lot of emotion behind those dark eyes, don't you think?"

"A lot of strength and a love of beauty," Laura finished off. "I've decided he's a man of strong passions but they're clamped down tight."

"That makes sense when one is trying to get one's life back together. Kyall thinks Evan's a man who has removed himself from some crisis situation. We'd all like to know what, but Evan's not talking. I suppose he will when he's ready. The Outback isn't his world."

"It's offering him solace," Laura offered. "Like me."

"I'm pleased to say you've lost that look of stress," Sarah approved. In fact, Laura looked glowing.

"I do feel better. More relaxed. It's comforting to know Evan Thompson is right next door. All six-four of him. He's taken on the role of big brother."

"Does that bother you?"

"No. It's a bit of a game we're playing. He doesn't want to see me as a woman; he prefers to see me as a mixed-up teenager. Fewer complications."

"You still haven't been able to approach the subject of Colin?" Sarah watched Laura as a friend and as a doctor.

"I've answered quite a few of Evan's questions, but no. My spirit is healing, especially when I look up at the Outback

stars at night. the sheer numbers, the brilliance and the closeness. I don't want thoughts of Colin to slow the process. As
for Evan, I have to think he's very much at home interview-
ing people.''

"A Pulitzer Prize winner?" Sarah suggested with a smile.

"It wouldn't surprise me. It wouldn't surprise me either to
find out his name is something quite different from
Thompson.''

"I suppose if he doesn't tell us one day we'll stumble on
his identity,'' Sarah said. "One thing we can be sure of—
he's a man of integrity. One recognizes the quality right off.''

"You look so happy, Sarah.'' Laura was struck by her
friend's incandescence. "Radiant would have to say it. And
Kyall mirrors your happiness. I'm so glad for you both.' She
remembered her manners. "Could I get you something?" She
half rose in anticipation. "Tea, coffee, a cold drink?''

"No, thanks, Laura.'' Sarah waved her back into her
chair." Kyall and I have many things to attend to. A trip to
Wunnamurra is first on the agenda. I can't stay long but I
wanted you to hear my news, then I'm off. It will all be
public soon enough.''

"Okay, I'm all ears.'' Laura leaned forward, feeling a tremendous sense of kinship with this beautiful woman.

"It's altered everything—our whole lives, our plans—but
we're thrilled about it.'' Sarah's expression was exalted.

"So tell me?'' Laura pleaded. "I can't stand the suspense.
I recognized something wonderful had happened to you the
moment you danced through the door.''

"That's it! I feel like I'm walking on air. Do you believe
in God?'' she asked Laura, very earnestly.

"I do.''

"So do I now. I wasn't sure. You're going to be stunned.''

"If it makes you look this good, stun away.''

Even then Laura couldn't begin to take in the story Sarah
began to unfold.

In the quietness of the afternoon Sarah told of the close
childhood bond between her and Kyall McQueen, of the op-
position from Kyall's family, most significantly Kyall's

grandmother, Ruth McQueen, the family matriarch. The result of that intense relationship—an unplanned pregnancy when she was still at school.

Before Laura could recover, Sarah swept on. "Needless to say Ruth was beside herself with anger and outrage. I wasn't going to be allowed to ruin Kyall's life. I understood that. My own life would be for ever changed, but Ruth had no concern about that. I was so young. Mum and I didn't have much, only each other. I was terrified that what Ruth was saying was the truth. The McQueens have always been regarded as very special people. They practically own the town. My father—he died early—used to work on the station as a shearer. There was no question of a serious relationship, let alone a match."

"So what happened?" Laura was finding it unbelievable that the serene, composed Sarah had been caught up in such drama.

"Ruth bundled me off to a little coastal town to wait for the birth. She wanted me to have an abortion, but I refused. When the shock of finding I was pregnant settled, I wanted my baby. I held her for a few minutes after she was born. She was perfect. Ruth told me the next morning my baby had died."

"Ah, Sarah!" Laura felt the shock right through her system.

"But she didn't die," Sarah told her friend quickly, seeing the stricken expression on Laura's sensitive face. "Ruth McQueen deceived me. She deceived my mother. Kyall was never told."

"But that's monstrous!" Laura understood instantly. "It puts my story into perspective. You must hate her? To do something like that— But how?"

"Cold-bloodedly and without a moment's thought for what her actions were going to do to me. My baby was exchanged with an infant who did die of respiratory problems. Ruth paid a nurse to make the change."

"Sarah, what can I say? I can scarcely believe this."

"It's all true." Sarah gave a short laugh. "It could easily

have remained true, only for the grace of God. Kyall and I
have only now discovered our daughter. As fate would have
it she's staying on a schoolfriend's property for the holidays.
I was called to a very serious accident on the property that
turned out to be fatal. Kyall and I went back to the homestead
for a cup of tea, and our daughter walked into our lives.
Living proof after years of hell.''

"But how did you know?" Laura's voice reflected her
stunned emotions.

"Laura, she's the image of me," Sarah said simply. "The
woman who took her home and reared her, very successfully,
is the same woman who was in the small maternity hospital
with me. I've never forgotten her name. Stella. Stella
Hazelton. It was Stella's little baby who died. But Fiona's
our daughter, Laura. We want her.''

"Of course you do." Laura's reaction was strong. "It's so
sad, though. It will involve—''

"Pain for the 'parents' who reared her?" Sarah spoke out
as Laura hesitated. "That's the hard part. The Hazeltons did
a fine job. For that we'll be everlastingly grateful. Fiona has
been very loved and Fiona loves them. Why wouldn't she?
Her parentage was never in question. Until now. Fiona is our
daughter. Kyall's and mine. We missed the first fifteen years
of her life, irreplaceable years, but we're not missing the rest.
Between us all we came to a decision Fiona should come to
us, her true parents. That will happen when she's ready to
make the adjustment. Oh, Laura, she's perfectly beautiful.''
Sarah's velvet-brown eyes filled with emotional tears.

"If she's like you she must be." Laura leaned over and
squeezed Sarah's hand. "This is a truly amazing story.''

"In confidence, for the moment.''

"Of course. I won't breathe a word.''

"It will get around soon enough. Harriet knows. I never
did feel in my deepest being my baby had died.''

"And Kyall? You never told him?''

"I know what you're thinking. He should have been told.''
Sarah's eyes darkened.

"I'm making no judgements, Sarah,'' Laura answered at

once. "I don't know the circumstances but I do know you must have been subjected to tremendous emotional stress. You thought you'd lost a child. The greatest grief a woman can suffer."

Sarah's golden head was downbent. "The shock has been greatest for Kyall. I've lived with the loss of my baby for half my lifetime. Kyall never knew he had a child. I thought I was sparing him the agony. That's my only explanation. He took it very hard. I don't think he'll ever get over it—except we have our daughter."

"But what of his grandmother? Are you going to confront her?"

"This very day." Sarah's musical voice turned uncharacteristically harsh.

"Oh, Sarah! It will be a ghastly business."

"I'm sure. But Judgement Day is at hand for Ruth McQueen. Kyall has been very close to her all his life. He's the one person in the world Ruth loves. All the rest are peripheral figures. But there are different kinds of loving."

To men like Colin it meant possession, Laura thought. Ownership of a woman's body and mind.

"Ruth's brand of loving is destructive," Sarah said. "While she proclaimed her great love of her grandson she robbed him of his child. She feels no remorse. That's the sort of woman she is."

Laura had to look away. "How very strange."

"Strange doesn't say it, Laura. When Ruth McQueen is crossed she becomes a devil."

Laura had some experience of devils.

It had taken many years for Sarah to deal with her traumas. By the grace of God they were in the past. Now it's my turn, Laura thought. If Sarah could live with the hell of a lost child, survive and become a fine doctor, surely she could change the terrible mess she had made of her life by marrying Colin.

One didn't become strong overnight, not after all the awful fear she'd been living with, but there was some magic about this town. The very sunlight had healing power. The friendliness of its people. A woman like Sarah. Evan. She had come to depend on his friendship. Since coming to Koomera Crossing her life had irrevocably changed course.

CHAPTER SIX

THE morning session was going surprisingly well for him. The words flowed. He was able to report on some of the most terrible events of his life as though he were writing a book of horrors to be turned into a war movie. For the first time he was able to stand back from the terrible stress, subdue his anger, while he captured scenes of the days and nights when madness had reigned.

The phone rang.

Damn! Sometimes he wanted to rip it out of the wall. His agent, George Costello, was really pushing him, trying to get him to agree to a deadline. He was taking calls from Channel Nine. They wanted him to cover world events. Badly, it seemed. They liked his style, his narration, the direct way he approached a story.

The TV channel were talking big money—not that money had ever driven him. He had more than enough, mostly inherited from his dead father. He would gladly give it away to have his father back. It was clear to him now his peers had judged him and found he had made a significant contribution.

"You made a terrific impact, Evan, with your reportage from the front line," Costello was fond of telling him.

And the life had made a big impact on him.

He spoke gruffly into the phone. "Evan Thompson." Thompson had been the name of his father's driver: a good loyal friend, in the wrong place at the wrong time.

A woman's cultured mature voice, still retaining its English accent, was on the other end. "Harriet, here, Evan."

He apologized wryly. "Sorry, Harriet, if I barked. I was preoccupied with something. It's easy to lose the thread."

"That's all right, Evan." Harriet sounded as if she had more important matters to discuss. "I have some disturbing news, I'm afraid. I've just had a distressed call from Sarah. Ruth McQueen has gone missing. They're searching for her now."

He went to say something. Caught himself. "Surely she hasn't gone off into the bush by herself? That's a strange thing for a woman of her age and experience to do. Even if she thinks she knows it like the back of her hand it's still possible to become disoriented in the wilderness. She may have taken ill. Had a fall. What exactly happened?"

It took Harriet a moment to answer. "It's difficult to tell it all, Evan. You'll be hearing most of it soon enough. The family is fairly frantic. Ruth has been a most difficult woman—" God, what an understatement, Harriet thought "—but she is the matriarch, and she's well into her seventies."

"Is it possible she has a hidden agenda?" he couldn't help asking. "I can't imagine her wandering off, Harriet. If ever a woman had her wits about her it's Ruth McQueen."

"Ah, yes!" Unconsciously Harriet's tone turned bone-dry. "Nevertheless, she's nowhere in the homestead or the main compound. Now they're searching the bush."

"All those lagoons and waterholes!" He had a strange feeling in the pit of his stomach. "It's to be hoped no harm has come to her. Do they need help?"

Harriet's tone warmed. "Thank you, Evan, but they have enough men on the ground. Kyall has taken the helicopter up. What I'd like you to do, if you would, is pass on the news to Laura. She doesn't know Ruth of course, but she does know Kyall and Sarah. I couldn't be more pleased she has you for a neighbour."

"Why, Harriet?" he gently challenged. Harriet the matchmaker.

There was a pause. "Because I am."

"I'll go next door right now, Harriet. Could you ring me if there's any news?"

It sounded as though Harriet had sucked in her breath. "To be truthful, Evan, I can't think the news will be good," she said.

*   *   *

When he went next door to the cottage he found Laura in the rear garden, clipping back the swaying heads of lavender that had turned sea-blue in the hot sun. They smelled wonderfully, but were encroaching on the brick path.

He'd got into the habit of glancing through a side window to see if she was working in the garden. Somehow the sight she made, like a beautiful Renoir painting, eased his soul. Today she was wearing a pastel pink T-shirt tucked into narrow jeans with a fancy belt with a big turquoise medallion around her tiny waist. On her head, protecting her luminous skin, she wore a large straw hat, the romantic kind, its wide brim floppy with full-blown fabric roses; soft leather shoes were on her feet.

All the world gilded, he thought. Pulsing with heat waves that released all the dry aromatic scents of the bush. Songbirds sang from the trees, softening the excited squawks of the brilliantly plumaged lorikeets as they plundered the grevillea brushes. Bees droned. So peaceful. So paintable.

His own country had to be the safest place in the world, he thought. Australia. New Zealand. Neither had experienced war and bloodshed on their soil. Neither had been exposed to the terrible sights and sounds that had affected him so deeply. Such safety was to be treasured.

As he stood staring at her she suddenly realized he was there. "Hello, Evan," she called, so sweetly he could feel his body stir. He hadn't had a woman in quite a while, but he knew in his heart he wanted this woman even as his mind told him she was untouchable. "Have you come along to help me?" she asked, teasingly.

"Of course not." Only then could he move, sauntering down to her. "It's glorious work, puttering about a garden. Besides, how can you learn if I do it all for you?"

"You're saying I'm used to having a gardener?" She tilted her head right back to look up at him, and the thought came out of nowhere that she loved his face. The sculptured head, the large handsome features, the square jaw and those black eyes that were resting on her. Could their depths ever be trawled?

He picked a paper daisy and pretended to feel the texture before he reached out to lift her to her feet. What would it be like to kiss her mouth, so beautiful, so tender? Cup her face with his hands... "Didn't you?" he asked sardonically.

She walked into the trap. "I wasn't allowed to make mistakes, Evan."

It wasn't the answer he'd expected. He stared at her, perturbed. "Surely we can't be talking about your parents?" Daddy's Little Girl? Some daddies were terribly possessive of their beautiful little girls, he thought.

She shrugged, wiped the tips of her fingers on her jeans before she accepted his hand. "Stop trying to catch me out, Evan Thompson. Okay, so what brings you here? I know. You want morning tea? You're crazy about my little Anzac biscuits?"

He gave a short laugh. "That's true. Like most men, I have a sweet tooth. But why don't you come inside? I know you've got that shady hat to protect you—it looks very fetching, by the way—but this Outback sun packs a lot of punch."

"You're telling me." She looked up at him, registering the expression in those brilliant dark eyes. "What is it, Evan?" she questioned, anxiety stirring.

"You're a hard person to keep things from."

"You look as though you have something you wish to say."

"Perhaps inside," he said.

She could feel herself start to tremble, her limbs weak. "Something about me?"

"God, no!" His black brows drew together. "I'm sorry, Laura. I didn't intend to alarm you. It's not about you at all."

"Oh!" She couldn't prevent the deep sigh of relief.

"You're full of fears, aren't you?" His eyes swept her. He wanted to pull her to him, lend her some of his own abundant strength.

She swallowed back the emotion in her throat. "I guess our fears follow us wherever we go."

"Until we turn and confront them."

"Believe me, I will," she said, seized by hope that hadn't

existed before. Even so, it was a terrible thing to live with the fear that Colin would rather kill her than see her happy with someone else. "But I need time."

"Okay." His eyes remained steady on hers. Moments stretched out. Too long. There was sexual attraction. Astonishing, mysterious, powerful.

It was Laura who took a little step back, blinking to break the spell. He was so compelling, so at ease within his own body. His whole aura flowed over her.

"I'll wash my hands in the laundry," she said quickly. "Why don't you go into the house?"

"Maybe I'll put coffee on." He started to move off with long strides. He knew he could fluster her very easily, but he was loath to make her feel threatened in any way. Secrecy surrounded Laura as he supposed it surrounded him.

"I'd like a cup," she called.

He was grinding the coffee beans—good beans, a present from him—when she came in the back door, quietly removing the big straw hat. She was the classic romantic heroine, with her sensitivity and her lovely dreamy face.

"You want it straight?" he asked.

"Unless it's terrible news, Evan. Nothing about Sarah or Kyall." Her green eyes were registering concern.

"No," he hastened to reassure her. "It's about Ruth McQueen. She's disappeared."

"Disappeared?" She looked across at him in astonishment. "From where? The homestead—Wunnamurra? Sarah was only there yesterday."

"I'll tell you what I know." He began to measure the coffee into the pot. "Harriet Crompton rang me. She and Sarah are very close, as you know. It appears fears are held for Mrs McQueen's safety. She's nowhere in the main compound. They're searching the bush."

"Oh, how dreadful!" Laura slumped into the curved banquette, wondering if this new development had something to do with yesterday's confrontation.

"Has something occurred to you?" He shot her a razor-sharp glance.

"Me? What would I know?" she evaded. "I've never even met Mrs McQueen, but I've certainly had time to gather she's an extraordinary person."

"A real tyrant. But something flickered in your eyes." God knew he was getting to know her face intimately. "I couldn't help noticing Sarah paid you a visit yesterday afternoon. Her car was out front."

"She naturally wanted to see what I was making of the place. With your help, as I told her. I'm very grateful."

"People like us should stick together," he said sardonically, thinking an army of men would be tripping over themselves trying to help her. "Anyway, that was the message as relayed by Harriet. Sarah wanted you to know. Apparently they're all very upset."

"I don't like the sound of this, Evan," she said, understanding her friend Sarah's relationship with Ruth McQueen wasn't good.

"What do you think has gone wrong?" He assembled cups, saucers, spoons, cream and sugar. He knew the place as well as she did.

"Why would a woman like Ruth McQueen wander off?" Laura propped her elbow on the table, supporting her white brow with her hand. "Maybe she needed a place to think?"

"So far away no one would ever find her?" he asked dryly.

"What do you mean?"

"I'm not sure. We haven't heard the whole story, Laura. Gossip here and there. A warning. Don't ever get caught by Ruby Hall. Someone ought to caution her. She's dreadfully reckless with the truth."

"That's the town sticky beak? I picked that up from Harriet."

"Be on your guard. I can promise you she'll be on your case."

"Won't do her much good." Laura smiled. "I can be as determinedly non-forthcoming as you."

"Not possible, Laura." That beautiful rare smile again.

"I won't argue. But thanks for the tip. I'll know to steer clear of Ruby without making an enemy of her."

"Good." He didn't crowd her, but went to the opposite end of the banquette. It was too damned cramped anyway, especially for a man his size. "There aren't supposed to be secrets in bush towns. Ruth McQueen from all accounts is a ruthless woman. Not liked at all, while Kyall is universally admired. Mrs McQueen is vehemently against Sarah, as I imagine you know. She idolizes her grandson. Sarah and Kyall have just become engaged and the balance of power has shifted. Dictators don't like that."

"No," she replied briefly, her mind never far from Colin. "Perhaps she's trying to scare them by vanishing?" Laura tested her idea on him.

"Emotional blackmail, do you mean? She *could* take that approach," he said dubiously. "On the other hand a woman like that must feel she's in total control."

She had experience of the rage when a controller like Colin didn't feel that way. "It doesn't sound good," Laura offered sombrely.

"No."

"Sarah was so very, very happy yesterday. I would hate that to change."

"So would I. Sarah deserves to be happy. It's time for her to be."

"It doesn't sound as though she could be happy living at the McQueen homestead with that very grand lady who'll do anything to upset her."

"Kyall won't let that happen. I'm sure all will be resolved."

"Sadly, life's not always like that."

"Don't fall into the doldrums. Eat that biscuit," he said. "You haven't put on an ounce."

Her expression lightened. "What was it the Duchess of Windsor used to say?"

"One can't be too rich or too thin," he answered.

"Being rich doesn't ensure happiness," she said.

"No, it doesn't. The first time I saw you I thought you were a poor little rich girl with a tale to tell."

"I know."

"You do come from a privileged background?"

"You surely don't want me to apologize for it?"

He shook his head. "Of course not. I was one of the lucky ones myself. But I would like to hear what you're holding back. It's hard to believe a too-demanding boyfriend could cause you such grief."

Why couldn't she say it? It's my husband. He's brutal by nature, with darkness in him. "You don't know what I'm dealing with, Evan," was all she could manage at the time.

"Tell me." He caught her fingers briefly, felt their tremble.

"Maybe I don't want you to see me as I am." It came out so very starkly she herself was shocked.

"If you're trying to tell me you've done bad things in your life, I just don't believe it."

"Not bad things, no." God, she hoped not. Was it bad to have allowed Colin to rape her? For that was what it had been. No love. No consent. But she couldn't have stopped him without being knocked senseless.

"In retrospect I can see how naïve I've been. I don't admire myself for it. I've accepted people at face value. If they were nice to me I thought they were nice people. But some wear handsome masks to hide their ugly faces. Maybe they're really devils, or in the devil's employ? That's when despair comes."

The mere thought of her entangled with a "devil" chilled his blood. Goodness knew, he'd seen the face of evil in a beautiful woman. "Laura, if you're in a bad situation you have to get free," he said, with some passion.

She closed her eyes. "I know that. I'm working on it. I don't feel alone. But I need a little time." Why couldn't she simply say, Something horrible happened to me, Evan. A marriage that shamed me. She didn't realize that hers was a classic response from innocent victims of abuse.

"Did you live with this man?" Evan asked bluntly, giving

in to his first bitter taste of something near jealousy. He
hated it.

Her beautiful clear eyes became shuttered. "He told me
he loved me. He swore it time after time."

"It sounds more like he terrorized you." His voice was
grim.

Laura shook her head, not ready to tell anyone outside
Sarah, another woman, what she had suffered at Evan's
hands. "I just fell out of love with him." She took a quick
sip of her coffee, swallowed it.

"Are you sure of that?"

"Haven't I come here to escape?"

"Obviously he has a powerful hold on you?"

"Yes." No point in lying.

"Laura, I'm sorry."

She couldn't fail to recognize his sincerity. "I'm sorry too.
But it's my own fault. I was the easiest target." She wondered what he would ask next.

"You know, you're the one who has to decide you need
help. Or do you want to deliver yourself back to him."

"God, no!" She couldn't stop the shudder. "What an unbearable thought. But he won't let go." In fact I'm certain
he's already begun looking, she thought.

"That might well be the case with you?" he watched her
face. "You can't let go either."

"That's not right, Evan," she said, very quietly, her soft
lovely features firming with resolve.

"Then help is at hand, Laura. All you have to do is want
it."

"You have no use for weak people, do you?" She lifted
her head.

"I don't regard you as weak. Whatever makes you think
that?"

"I'm not a woman of substance." She fought against sudden tears.

"I'd like to be—I'm going to be—a woman of substance,
like Sarah," she said.

"Sarah has had her troubles, I'm sure. And they've left

their mark on her. As my bad experiences have left an in-
delible mark on me. You're younger than either of us. One
doesn't know everything at twenty or twenty-three. That's no
age at all! One's whole life is a process of learning. Obviously someone has gone out of their way to try to crush your
spirit. After your father died you must have felt very much
alone."

"I really needed him." She forced her grip on her coffee
cup to relax. "I don't think I've felt safe for years. Certainly
for a long time now the feeling of safety has eluded me."

"What drew you to your doctor, then?". he asked, using
a quiet, soothing voice. "Why did you fall in love with
him?"

She put a hand beneath her satin hair. "He's very handsome. Nothing like you."

"Thank you." His mouth turned down.

"I mean he's an entirely different type. Golden-haired. Azure blue eyes. Cold, cold, cold. Nowhere near as tall as you,
or so powerfully built. He's slim. Very elegant, in his way.
He's terribly interested in clothes. He wears only the best."

"These are very superficial things, Laura," he chided her.

"You asked. I'm trying to answer. He's clever. He's very
highly regarded."

"What's his speciality?"

"I'm not saying. I've already told you too much. He's very
much admired."

"It occurs to me *you* don't admire him." His deep voice
was dry.

"He's so clever he can be insufferable," she burst out,
then stopped abruptly. "That's all I'm telling you, Evan."

"Well, it's a start." He continued to study her expressive face.

"I don't buy *your* cover either," she countered. "I'm going to steal into your place one day…"

"To do what?" He narrowed his eyes at her.

"Search for clues. You could be an international spy. Are
they still around?"

"Of course they are," he confirmed. "They're all out there

in the arena. All the major powers, all the little guys spying on each other. The most extraordinary thing is even if they're on the same side they won't tell each other what they've learned. The strongest intelligence agencies just don't want to share.''

"That sounds dangerous."

"Worse, it could be criminal negligence."

"You've travelled widely?" It was good to shift the focus from herself.

"I have. A lot of the time hitching rides. Moving on."

"An adventurer?"

"Something like that."

"Why did you move here? It's not your environment. You couldn't be more isolated."

"That was the big attraction," he said dryly. "The isolation and the lure of the desert. Though the desert was nearly the death of me."

"How? Please go on." She was fascinated.

"I was with an anthropologist friend who was visiting sacred sites when our helicopter crashed. One minute we were sitting pretty, the next falling out of the sky. This is it! It's all over! The pilot was badly injured, but Greg and I managed to get him clear before the chopper exploded. Search and Rescue spotted us."

"A bad experience."

"I've had worse." And a lot closer, he thought.

"There must have been some good ones?" she insisted, admiring the way his thick dark hair curled around his head and onto his nape.

"Many beautiful and unforgettable ones. The heavenly peaks of the Himalayas. I didn't climb. I took it easy in a chopper. And perhaps the most awesome journey was to Antarctica, some years back." Hell, would she remember his photograph on the back cover of his book, complete with full beard? "I got to see a glorious world with a group of great guys from all over," he continued briskly. "In a curious way the vastness, the overwhelming feeling of being a speck, alone in its powerful effect, isn't unlike the feeling one gets in the heart of the Outback. You recognise how tough it is to survive. The huskies howl as mournfully as any dingo. The thought that one could easily lose one's life is the same in both places."

"Which makes us full of admiration for all our explorers."

"Lord, yes," he agreed fervently, even reverently. "It's not a question of pushing to the limits. It's going beyond human endurance. And the beauty of the place! The Outback is all brilliant oven-baked ochres. Extremes of colour—blood-red, cobalt blue, the rich gold of the Spinifex plains. A world of great heat and dancing mirage. Antarctica is blinding whiteness. A world of ice with tinges of aqua in the crevices. From the great red pyramids of the desert, its shifting sands sculpted by the winds, to the frozen pyramids of ice and the swirling white blizzards."

"I'm forming instant pictures." Laura shivered. "How long were you there?"

"A little over two weeks, then I had to move on." He didn't say he'd been due back in Washington.

"I would think an experience like that would not only be memorable it would stay for ever."

"Like a space flight to the moon." He smiled.

"I'm surprised you haven't been there." she gently mocked.

"I've talked to a guy who has."

"Truly?"

He nodded, turning his head as a familiar strident sound interrupted them. "That's the phone. I'll get it, if you like. It could be Harriet. I asked her to ring us if she had news."

"I pray it's good!"

CHAPTER SEVEN

THE shock of Ruth McQueen's death immediately encompassed the whole town, although no one was informed of the exact circumstances. The official word was heart attack.

The fact that she had gone for a long walk in the bush no one found extraordinary. Ruth McQueen, after all, had run a great Outback station almost single-handedly for many years after her husband's premature death. She had led a full and active life, in her youth and middle life having piloted her own plane over the vast wilderness that was the country's Red Heart.

Ruth McQueen was the Outback like few other women, the matriarch of a great pioneering family. What everyone did consider extraordinary was she had gone off on her own without telling anyone. A grave mistake in the bush. Even seasoned stockmen had found themselves lost.

But Ruth McQueen, paradoxically respected and loathed, had been a bold woman, and appropriately she had died boldly, perhaps wishing to end her life out in the wild bush rather than in her bed. For it was soon made public that Ruth McQueen had had a heart condition she had been advised would kill her if she persisted in living her life to extremes.

One would have needed to know Ruth McQueen and her family intimately to begin to understand the true circumstances that had led to her death. But, as with most things pertaining to powerful families' affairs, the exact truth would never be known. It would do no good. Rather, a lot of harm—which was why the McQueen family reached a unanimous agreement to bury the matriarch with the full honours they all knew she did not deserve.

It was called burying Ruth with her sins. But first the family had to come together in solidarity. Perpetuate a myth.

Kyall's younger sister, Christine, a glamorous international model, would be asked to return home. No one was absolutely sure she would. The late Ruth McQueen had to take much of the blame for her granddaughter's defection.

The shoot had actually begun with a crew call at six o'clock in the morning. Christine had had to be on the set by eight o'clock for hair and make-up. The photographer, a famous one, favoured working early mornings or late afternoons. This was a big budget shoot to launch a French designer's new collection of trousers, trouser suits, evening tuxedos and smoking suits with the waistcoats, shirts and blouses that went with them.

Christine had been engaged for the project because she looked fabulous in trousers. She had a tall, ultra-lean, sexy body. Add to that she was beautiful, with a healthy vivacious look that was gaining ground against the anorexic waifs. She had gorgeous blue eyes and that wonderful lavish hair. She was also intelligent, co-operative, good humoured, and clever enough to come up with many different looks. A winning recipe for becoming a success.

Christine had never dreamed about success when she had fled her home, the historic sheep station Wunnamurra in the Australian Outback. Her flight had been to escape her mother's and her grandmother's domination.

By sixteen she had grown into a frame inherited from her father's side of the family—nearly six feet tall, with wide shoulders, a shapely bust, lean through the torso and flanks, and long, long legs. Her mother was short of stature, like her grandmother. They made up for it with their lofty, commanding manner.

Both had been uncomfortable with the fact Christine had grown ''so big''. They did not find it attractive. It was splendid for brother Kyall, the McQueen heir, to top six-three; disaster for a young woman. Men would treat her with wry amusement. Women would either be sympathetic or cruel.

Christine's height and her weight—she had been much heavier then—had made her mother especially very unhappy. Her mother had never mentioned her now famous smile, or her perfect teeth which had landed her a lucrative toothpaste ad in the early days. Her mother had despaired—and had been quite vocal: Christine would never find a man who could sweep her off her feet. She'd survived on the love of her father and the brother she adored.

On her eighteenth birthday she had been able to access the income from her trust fund. It had provided her with the means for escape. She would live where she chose; be her own woman. She had started in Sydney where a top model agency, instantly seeing her potential, had taken her on to their books, promising her big things if she'd follow their advice. She had—to the letter.

A short year later she had moved with their blessing to New York, where things had really begun to happen.

A few months back she'd even been offered a feature role in a big budget action film, but when it was all said and done her life, exotic and crammed to the brim with her choice of endless parties and functions, wasn't making her as happy as her fans might have thought. Neither was her succession of relationships.

All her life, from adolescence, what she'd wanted to do was get married and settle down with her prince—her golden-headed blue-eyed Mitch. Mitchell Claydon, heir to Marjimba Station. She'd always loved Mitch, as Kyall had loved Sarah.

God knew Kyall had been through hell for years because Sarah had chosen a career as a doctor over becoming Kyall's wife. Clever Sarah! Sarah had been a good friend to her when they were kids. Sarah had never laughed unkindly.   Sarah had always told her that one day, when her looks settled, she was going to be so beautiful.

"It will happen, Chris!"

Sarah had been beautiful even as a kid. She remembered the great bond that had existed between Sarah and her brother; between her and Mitch.

So here I am at the high point of my career, and nowhere near as happy with my life as I should be, Christine thought as someone knocked, then pushed open the door of her trailer—her home on the set. She and Sylvie Chadwick, her favourite hairstylist, turned in mild surprise to see who it was.

"I thought we were supposed to be having a bloody break!" Sylvie exploded. "God knows, Chris is just a saint, putting up with bloody Malcolm's demands."

"It's not Malcolm. Not this time." Annie, one of the photographer's young assistants, apologised, grinding her hands together. She addressed the nicer-natured Christine directly. Sylvie was so fiery. Like her hair. "Sorry to barge in, Christine, but there's someone trying to get a message to you urgently. A lawyer, but I missed his name. Security wouldn't let him past. But here's a note." She produced a crumpled piece of paper that the protective Sylvie immediately snatched and passed to Christine unread.

"The amount of rubbish Chris has to put up with," Sylvie complained. "What's it say, Chris? Let me guess. He's a big fan? I can deal with it."

"Not this time, Sylvie," Christine said in a very quiet voice. "This is a message from home. From Australia."

"Bad news, luv?" Sylvie saw how Christine's colour had changed.

"I'm afraid so," Christine responded in the same quiet, unemotional voice. "My grandmother has died."

"Oh, that's rough!" The British-born Sylvie grasped Christine's shoulder sympathetically. "You never talk much about your life back in Oz, but I bet you loved her?"

"There was no one like her, actually."

"Ah, luv!" Sylvie, seared by images of her own darling grandmother, now passed away, quite missed the irony in Christine's voice.

No miraculous reconciliation there, Christine thought staring sightlessly at her own reflection. Even as she sought to take the news in she had to recognise that at this point in her life she wanted to go home. Not only to see her family.

Mitch would be there.

Laura let herself into the Endeavour Theatre, which also doubled as the concert hall, using the key Evan had given her.

After day after day of brilliant sunshine, cloudless cobalt blue skies, the quick silver of mirage, her eyes had to adjust to the gloom.

This was her second visit. She had spent most of yesterday afternoon practising, all her disciplines coming back to her as she had tried out the beautiful, very responsive piano. She was highly impressed with it. She would never have thought to find an instrument so fine in a small Outback town, but then McQueen money had provided it for the town and the McQueens apparently didn't do things by halves.

Tomorrow was Ruth McQueen's funeral. It had been set for mid-week, allowing time for Kyall's sister, Christine, their cousin Suzanne, a student in Sydney, and the extended family to arrive.

She still didn't know if she was going. She had no connection with the McQueens except through Sarah, who was marrying into the family. Though as far as the town was concerned she and Sarah were long-standing friends. Both of them had allowed the town to believe that. It was easier, and it had ensured Laura's quick acceptance. Evan thought she should go to support Sarah, and Evan was a very compelling man.

The interior of the theatre was very quiet and half dark, faintly musty from being closed up, almost ghostly, though the black grand piano had illuminated the moment she'd turned on some lights.

It was wonderful she'd been allowed access. She was very grateful and she owed it all to Evan. He had consulted the powers that be—Enid Reardon, Kyall's mother, the Mayor, and conductor of the town's orchestra guild, Alex Matheson.

Evan had told her Matheson was a brilliant musician who'd had to give up a promising career because of his erratic eyesight that sometimes left him half blind. A sad story and one that had really affected her. Evan said she would have her chance to thank Alex at the funeral, if she went along. It might seem strange if she didn't, given her friendship with Sarah.

She really didn't have any suitable clothes. Maybe she could find something.

The funeral was to take place at the McQueens' historic station Wunnamurra. Ruth McQueen was to be buried beside her husband in the family cemetery. She hadn't seen Sarah since it had happened, but they had spoken briefly on the phone. Sarah had sounded shocked, but strangely as though a great burden had lifted. Or so Laura had thought. She didn't really know what she had based that idea on. Nothing Sarah had actually articulated. More thoughts communicated through the mind.

Laura stared at the piano for a few moments without stirring. Then she went to it, opening it up, letting her fingers drift across the strings. No Colin to upset and undermine her, make her jittery with nerves. She sat down on the piano seat—she had already adjusted it—beginning to limber up with a technical exercise from her student days. That had been the best time of her life.

If only…if only…her father hadn't died. Her father would have seen through Colin's civilised exterior to the harshness beneath.

"My God, will you stop that?" Colin, venting his extreme irritation at her practice, his menacing undertone. "It's enough to make one plug one's ears. If you must play the piano, can't you choose something that falls a lot easier on the ear? Chopin, or something? Though your touch sounds to me all wrong. I'm shocked someone your size can make so much noise."

His opinion hadn't touched her. She was sure of her own gift. She had been judged by her peers. She knew Colin had no critical ear. His aim had been to paralyse her talent. The reason was simple. She must have no interest outside him.

Nevertheless, in no time at all she had learned not to play when Colin was around. It wasn't a good idea. She, who was full of music, had hungered for it, but had finally found herself shutting down her beautiful Kawai concert grand, turning the key. It had been her father's gift to her at age sixteen, after she had won a national concerto competition.

So her music had been silenced. Her dissenting voice silenced. Her spirit, if not broken, subdued. She had judged herself a total failure in her marriage. Of course that was what Colin had intended. He'd wanted her totally under his control.

She had prayed for help. Someone had listened. One liked to think of a guardian angel at times like that.

Why had she allowed herself to be so intimidated? Why had she crumbled under the weight of his hand? Why had she given him the twisted pleasure of her sob-strangled entreaties? She should have resisted and resisted. Become a warrior.

Perhaps been killed?

She had come to understand with a man like Colin it just could happen. Something could snap. Then the ambulance. The police. The shocked neighbours. How could anything like that have happened in such a house? To such beautiful people? With Colin's immaculate reputation it might even have been thought she had caused it, brought it all down on herself.

Abruptly Laura broke off the intricacies of the technical exercise she was performing on autopilot, allowing her hands to come to rest on the comforting keys. How she loved the feel of them, the pads of her fingers compulsively smoothing the surface. Such emotions washed through her when she played. Yet Colin had almost had her believing she was a woman who knew nothing about passion.

She understood her music thoroughly. She understood passion. What she hadn't understood was the terrible way Colin had tried to communicate passion through violence. Ugly raw violence.

In retrospect it shamed her deeply. Their marriage hadn't undergone a process of disintegration. There had been no marriage from day one. The rest had cast her into such a state of fear and deep confusion about her life that she had run. At the time she had thought of it as self-rescue. Now she knew she was as trapped as ever. She would never be free until she had confronted Colin.

That was definitely scary, but she was determined to

muster all her resources, and some she didn't know she had, to win this big battle in life.

It wasn't the time to think about it now, but how she'd feared that vein that had used to pump in Colin's temple. More often than not it had been the forerunner of some violent outburst against which she'd had no defence short of murder. Some men used their physical strength, so much superior to a woman's, to keep their womenfolk subdued. It was the highest form of cowardice.

She just couldn't imagine Evan Thompson raising his hand in anger to a woman. He would find that despicable. She had come to think of Evan as a mysterious dark knight who had come into her life when she so badly needed one. He stirred so much in her, enriching her mind and her spirit, though the rhythm that was beating and building up between them felt only too sexual.

The truth, and she had faced it, was that he attracted her powerfully. He both excited and calmed her—brought an awareness of herself as a woman she had never experienced with Colin. She loved the look of him—the sculptured features, the perfectly straight nose, the broad brow, the strong jaw, his mouth, his muscular frame. She loved his strength and the pile-up of energy that was in him, the sound of his deep voice.

She wondered if he knew how he affected her by the way she watched him. There was peril in that. It was the wrong time, even if all her emotions were right. She was a married woman, for all her marriage was a farce, but only half of her remembered that. The other half was fascinated by her neighbour. She loved the way he called out to her if he saw her in the garden. She loved the way their eyes met. After Colin's cold azure stare it was wonderful to burn herself in the eloquent beauty of a man's brilliant dark eyes.

She had to pull herself out of her abstraction. Keep her little fantasies to herself. She knew what her heart and body craved but it was far too dangerous. Her fingers began to move on the keys, selecting a Chopin nocturne at random...but it was predictably romantic.

*   *   *

She was not only technically brilliant, she was brilliantly expressive. He had known she'd be good. Even then she had surprised him. How foolish to assume because she was so small she couldn't produce a wonderful big tone.

He hadn't thought it a good idea to intrude on her yesterday, but he hadn't been able to resist the impulse to come today, virtually sneaking into the theatre by a side door.

She was so engrossed in a Rachmaninoff *étude* that went like the wind she didn't hear the slight noise made by the door. Just as well. He wanted to listen to her without her being aware of it. He wanted to look at her—God, had he ever seen a woman pianist look so beautiful?—without breaking her concentration or making her in any way self-conscious.

He knew everything she played until the little piece at the end. A mournful little piece that had him thinking of his father. The melody wound this way and that, circling like a lost bird, until it suddenly opened out, spreading its wings. It struck him that it was like a soul proceeding to heaven. He would have to ask her the name of the composer. He would have to ask her to play it again. She had a beautiful singing tone.

He moved unconsciously and immediately the spell was broken. His chair turned into a squeaking machine.

"Laura, I'm sorry," he called. "I was enjoying that so much."

She collected herself instantly, overcoming the inevitable moment of sheer panic. Would she ever be free of the anxiety? Even here?

"Evan!" She stood up, peering out into the gloom. "I can't believe I didn't hear you come in."

"You were too deep into the Rachmaninoff." He moved into the aisle, walking up towards the stage. "Want my opinion?"

"I really need more practice. I'm rusty."

"You're wonderful! That last piece broke my heart. What is it? I've never heard it before."

Her heart was a throb in her throat as she watched him

mount the stairs, slowly walk towards her. Careful, careful, she cautioned herself. Every time he looked at her it was as though a switch had been thrown, sparking a dazzle of lights. She couldn't look any more. She half turned away, touched the piano.

"Did it speak to you?" she asked.

"It did." He studied the way the soft colour rose to her cheekbones. "So sad—until the end, when it was absolutely transcending. I might have been watching a soul travelling to heaven."

She drew in a sharp breath, frankly fighting the urge to cry. "How extraordinary you should say that. I composed it in memory of my father. I loved him so much. I wanted to express it. He was a good man. A fine man. I felt if anyone deserved a reward when life was over he did."

There's a limit to what a man can take, he thought. Something about her was restoring his faith in life. He wanted to hold her hand. It was a beautiful hand. The same hand that had an extraordinary affinity with the keyboard. Now it seemed she was a composer.

"That's almost silenced me, Laura," he said gently, thinking of the great love he'd had for his own father, so tragically and traitorously cut down. "How very gifted you are."

"If only I could lay all my sorrows to rest that way."

There was a haunting little smile on her mouth. Not the slightest hint of sexual provocation, yet he found it intoxicating. He dug his hands in his pockets in case he reached for her, pulled her into the shelter of his arms, dipping his head so he could cover her mouth with his own.

"You seem to have an infinite capacity for feeling pain. Probably as a musician it's inherent. Then again, something has happened to you to cause a lot of damage."

"You really wouldn't want to know, Evan." Quietly she closed the keyboard.

"I think I would." He moved to lower the heavy lid for her.

"Thank you."

"You're welcome. I take it the recital is over?"

"I've been playing for quite a while. One day you might hear my life story, I promise."

"Not now?" he asked quietly.

"I have to get clear in my mind what to tell you."

"You mean you're going to edit it? Cut out the bits that might be of vital importance?"

"You've not told me your story either," she countered. "I haven't heard about your life."

"Why would you care?"

"For all you know I might care an awful lot," she surprised him by saying. "You've been very kind to me, Evan. I have a sense of security when you're around, like a shining shield. I'm very grateful to you too for arranging for me to practise like this. I hadn't expected such a beautiful instrument."

"Just about the best. As soon as Harriet finds out how gifted you are you'll be roped in for concerts."

"Oh, no!" She brushed a nervous hand down the lilac cotton skirt that she wore with a matching cotton and lace camisole. She'd quickly found she had to dress for the heat.

"Are you a nervous performer?" he asked, with a quirk of the brow.

For a big strong man he could be unbearably sweet. "Who isn't?" She shrugged.

"Too nervous to go on? I did know a very good cellist who was too nervous to perform in public. Just among friends. Fellow musicians."

"I can understand that." It was easier than saying she couldn't possibly draw public attention to herself. Easier than saying that before her marriage she had performed many times in public. Always nervous, but focused the instant her hands touched the keys.

"But you could play for me?"

His deep voice touched a chord. "I have. You're a very good listener."

"On the contrary, I can't listen unless the performer is special."

"I guess I'm a bit like that too. One knows perhaps too much about it. The critical faculty is always in place."

He nodded. "What about a coffee?"

"I'd like that." She turned to hunt up the keys to the theatre. "The little coffee shop with the pink and white ruffled curtains? It has such a cheerful atmosphere."

"Then Pamela's it is. We might as well go out the side door. It's easier."

"I'll turn off the lights."

"Right." He walked down the short flight of steps to the auditorium, waiting for her to join him.

On stage, Laura threw the switch, at the same time making the mistake of staring up at the blinding dazzle of lights. They immediately left an afterburn on the retina.

"Laura?" he called up to her, seeing the way she closed her eyes and turned her head.

"I'm okay." In fact she felt a little foolish. It was an inadvertent thing. The black dots didn't go away quickly, but she found herself stepping off the stage. Her vision slowly cleared, though she wasn't altogether sure of her footing.

"Lord!" Her every nerve jumped. She gave an involuntary little cry as the heel of her sandal caught. "Evan, I'm sorry, but I can't see where I'm going."

"I'm here. Right here," he called reassuringly, moving swiftly into position at the base of the steps. "You shouldn't have looked up at the lights."

"No, that was stupid. Oh, God! I'm going to fall." She had instant visions of a sprained ankle.

"No, you're not!"

The next moment she was locked securely in his arms, her feet dangling clear of the floor.

The whole world jolted to a stop. It was like coming into a safe harbour after a storm, though the air around them was full of motion.

Her mouth was a breath away from his chin. There was no fear. But excitement immeasurably beyond anything she had felt before. She wanted to stay like that for ever, embracing it. A dangerous way to feel, but it was out of her control.

"How did this happen?" His voice was very deep. He made no move to set her on her feet.

"I don't know. I'm embarrassed. That was stupid. I stumbled. You caught me."

"Okay, so we have an excuse." His voice was deep and exciting. There was an identical expression in his dark eyes. "It's just too damned hard not to kiss you, Laura."

"You mustn't," she whispered, at the same time raising her head, welcoming his kiss so much she could barely speak.

"I know I mustn't," he answered gently. "But that's not helping me right now. My God, what do you weigh? You're a featherweight. I could hold you like this until four in the morning."

Her green eyes were staring uncertainly into his, her lovely lips parted, her skin as white and soft as a gardenia, glowing in the dim light. He could feel the ache in his body. The need for a woman. Not any woman. Laura.

"This is what comes of being alone in the near dark," he said, drawing on all the gentleness in him. Inner wisdom told him Laura hadn't been treated with care. "Don't be frightened, Laura. I'd never hurt you."

"I'm not." Yet she instinctively braced herself from long habit. Waited. Other terrible kisses were coming back to her, the awful stroking of her white skin, the moments she'd tried desperately to escape. It was an involuntary thing thinking of Colin. Fear was always uppermost in her mind.

"Stop that," he said, very quietly.

"What am I doing?"

"Your whole body has gone tense."

Yet he held her so very tenderly. "It's just that—"

"Don't say anything unless it's the truth."

In one fluid movement he lowered her until her feet came to rest on the second step from the floor. Her head was almost level with his, which was just where he wanted it.

"Let yourself relax," he urged, his voice like black velvet.

"How can I?"

"You know I would never do anything to upset you."

She did know, and it was a revelation. Joy overtook apprehension. She felt her body might not be able to accommodate the extremity of her emotions. But any lingering fears were lost as he drew her against him, lowering his dark head until his mouth settled over hers.

Waves of desire came off him, giving her such a heady feeling of confidence in her womanliness that she was radiant with bliss. Colin's image disappeared.

Evan's kiss was so beautiful, so exciting, so wonderfully moving. She could feel her heart, so used to beating loud and hard with dread, simply melt. Warmth was like a beautiful, enveloping blush moving over her skin. What she was experiencing was flawless male mastery, yet it so wrapped her in multiple layers of security she abandoned herself entirely to the enormity of the moment.

Such an infinity of sensation piled up in her body. She felt her spirit soaring, as it did when she made music. She didn't flinch as the kiss deepened, became more passionate. She wasn't frigid at all. She could never think that of herself ever again. Not with Evan kissing her as if he was drowning in unimaginable delight, aching for her. She had become so accustomed to withholding response, but now that was impossible. With Evan she had cast off all barriers, in a world without horizons.

His strong fingers were in her hair, not tearing or pulling, but smoothing, as if its length was a precious bolt of silk. There was more than a good chance she might simply swoon away from such boundless tendresse.

"Laura?" He lifted his mouth from hers, aware she was striving to come up for air. He, himself, had never experienced such an extraordinary play of emotion. "You haven't gone to sleep?" he gently teased, luxuriating in her heavenly softness. Her fragrance all around him. Desire. Delight.

She let her head tip forward onto his chest, her whole body tingling from the contact. She could feel the warmth of his skin through his cotton shirt, smell his clean male scent, hear the thud of his heart. Her own heart was beating as if she'd just run one hundred metres.

"That wasn't so bad, was it?"

"Not a bit."

"Do you know how wonderful you are to kiss?"

"Am I?" She moved slightly so she could lay her cheek against him.

"Doesn't your peculiar boyfriend tell you that?"

"Don't let's talk about him," she begged. Colin had no place there.

"You didn't think of him when I was kissing you?"

She was truthful. "Only to realize I've never been kissed before," she said, her voice soft and intense.

"Then two kisses are surely better than one?"

How thrillingly quiet he was, yet his voice, his eyes, the way he looked at her, stirred her to her unguarded soul. It was a miraculous feeling, her body resting against his. She was getting such pleasure and comfort from it. What she'd said she meant. Evan's kiss was the only kiss she had received in her life.

"Come closer to me." He snuggled her supple, yielding body against him, everything that was tender in him aroused by the delicacy of her limbs.

"Evan?"

"It's only me."

If only she had never met Colin. But she had, and he had harmed her. She'd come a long way since then.

I can't let it go on like this with Evan. She spoke silently to herself. I must do something about it. I have to tell him the truth.

CHAPTER EIGHT

WUNNAMURRA Station was an island of civilisation in an ocean of Spinifex scorched to a bright gold. On their near two-hour journey from the town they had passed through an extraordinary landscape, making the trip to Wunnamurra for Ruth McQueen's funeral almost an adventure for the city-bred Laura.

"This is like being a million miles from anywhere," she said to Evan, who was doing the driving. "I thought I'd be looking at one of the world's harshest environments but this is more like a wonderland. All the fiery colours! Namatjira really did capture them." She gazed out of the window at the flying miles.

"These unique landscapes made him famous," Evan remarked of the famous aboriginal artist. "Even when he became a celebrity he always wanted to go home to the desert. So far as I'm concerned no one has been able to match him for capturing the essence of the Outback."

"And to think I used to consider the palette he used too vivid to be true," Laura confessed, "which shows my ignorance of the Outback. Just look at the red rocks, the red plains and dunes, the distant violet ranges all under the deepest blue sky I've ever seen. Not a single cloud. I love the ghost gums."

"Namatjira's 'ghostly gums' made his name. The silver-grey leaves, the crisp white branches and trunks. They're beautiful. Even the dead trees are marvelous, with their extraordinary gnarled shapes."

"What's that one over there?" Laura twisted her head around. "It's not a ghost gum." She pointed at a huge bare tree, its branches twisted into fantastic curves and angles.

"Desert Oak." Evan identified the species for her. "Casuarina decaisneana. How's that for a botany lesson?"

"Pretty good." She smiled. "I hope I'm not being a nuisance, asking all these questions, but what's the glitter in the distance?"

Evan eased the speed of his four-wheel drive so she could look her fill. "An area of gibber. Pebbles and stones, even boulders. They're rounded and polished by the windblown sand until they look like gems. That accounts for the glimmer. East of Lake Eyre is Sturt's Stony Desert. Now, that's a remarkable place. The surrounding plains are literally covered in colourful polished pebbles. The total effect is one of a never-ending mosaic."

How she was cherishing the trip, cherishing being with him, though half melancholy because she couldn't be indifferent to the fact she was still legally tied to Colin. She couldn't stop to analyse the exact feelings for Evan, especially since he'd kissed her. That would be like stepping off a cliff.

"Speaking of colour, you've had a colourful life?" She glanced at his bold sculptured face in profile, the strong column of his brown throat.

"I've seen a lot, Laura." He gave her back a glance. "A lot good. A lot bad. Australia is good. The Australian Outback is better. It's the heart and soul of the country. A healthy, healing environment—unless you're a complete fool and do the wrong thing, like heading off without telling anyone where you're going or travelling without water. Water is a very precious commodity out here."

"Even with all those interlocking watercourses, the lagoons and billabongs, the water running off all the rocks and gullies?" she asked.

"Providing one is near them," he pointed out dryly. "You've only seen the town. The bush is so vast you could have a thirty-kilometre walk in scorching sun. It doesn't take long to become severely dehydrated."

"One wonders why Mrs McQueen decided to venture out," Laura mused. "I understand she was an elderly woman."

"You'd never have known to look at her. She was all style.

An extraordinarily glamorous woman. Very black intelligent
eyes. A powerful woman too, but far from likeable as a lot
of powerful people are.'' he added dryly.

"Have you ever been anywhere there was a chance you'd
be killed?'' Laura startled him by asking.

He flicked a glance at her, very aware of how close she
was to him, inhaling her fragrance. "What a question.''

"Do you think you could answer it, oh, man of mystery?''

"I have to tell you I've been close to an active volcano.''
He gave her a half-smile. He could never tell her about his
perilous times in the Balkans.

"You're joking!''

"Not to mention all the poisonous gases in the air.''

"Where? Please do tell me?''

He smiled at the imploring note in her voice. "I was
twenty-five years old. In those days I thought nothing of taking risks. A friend of mine from my university days was a
geologist. Both of us were on holiday in Italy, fascinated with
volcanic eruptions. We decided to take off for Mount Etna.
The Viper, as the Italians call it.''

"What a scary thing to do!''

"You bet!'' he agreed mockingly. "In those days we
thought of it more an awe-inspiring adventure, and it was.
Small wonder some societies worship active volcanos.''

"And you actually stood on the edge of the crater?'' she
asked, fascinated.

"We did. But if you really want to see the earth's most
unique crater it's right here in the Red Centre. Actually, not
all that far away by charter flight. It's called Gosse's Bluff.
Spinifex plains just like these.'' He waved a hand at the rug-
ged landscape. "The pound roughly twenty, twenty-five kilometres across, surrounded by what appears to be a massive
circular range of mountains—which is, of course, the pink
sandstone wall of the crater. No one knows what caused the
mighty impact, comet or meteorite, but it must have been felt
all over earth. A cataclysmic explosion probably a couple of
hundred thousand times greater than the explosion that destroyed Hiroshima. Mercifully our scientists tell us huge

comet or meteorite falls like the one that created Gosse's
Bluff occur only once in a million years.''

''That's good to know,'' she shuddered wryly. ''I saw a
movie about a meteorite about to destroy earth not that long
ago. It was bad enough. Have you been to Gosse's Bluff as
well?''

In his other life he'd spent years globe-trotting, ready to
take off for an assignment at twenty-four hours' notice.
''No.'' His charismatic voice deepened. ''But if you'll come
with me I don't see any reason why we can't go. Vehicle
access is probably difficult. A helicopter could land.''

Laura felt her own cataclysmic jolt. ''Are you serious?''
Oh, let him be!

''Of course I'm serious. Would you like to go?''

The thought thrilled her unbearably. ''I'd love to go.''

''Well, then, the trip's on.'' He drank in her lovely face,
her excited response.

She'd told him the day before she didn't have a single
black outfit in her wardrobe to wear, but she'd found a very
stylish little navy suit which she wore with a white navy-
trimmed silk blouse beneath. It didn't take an experienced
eye to know it was top quality, very expensive. Her hair was
drawn back with a navy ribbon.

So young, so absolutely beautiful, so gifted. So why did
he think she was weeping inside? He realized his feelings for
her were growing into a private torment. What could come
of it? He didn't know where his life was heading. She was
clearly running from a serious situation. Now he had gone
and dreamed up this trip. Unsharable nights together under
the Outback stars. He had to be raving mad. Nevertheless, he
got himself in even deeper.

''We might as well take in Uluru,'' he added compulsively. ''Forget calling it Ayers Rock—Uluru is the only
name that calls up its mystery and magic. And twenty miles
on are the magnificent domes of Kata Tjuta.''

''The Olgas.'' She gave him a little smile.

''Both great monuments are sublime. Have you seen
them?''

"I haven't done anything much," she confessed. "I've never been further off-shore than New Zealand, Fiji, Bali. Once to Bangkok."

"Where did you stay?" He gripped the wheel as the four-wheel drive bounced over a very rough patch of low scrub.

"The Oriental."

"One of the great hotels of the world. So you weren't slumming it?" he observed dryly.

"Far from it." She dreaded saying the trip to Bangkok had been her honeymoon destination.

"You don't sound as though it was a wonderful experience. Surely the food alone is superb?"

"Of course it is. I loved the dazzlingly beautiful arrangements of flowers in the lobby. Great fish bowls on spectacular stands, filled with enough orchids or flowers in season to fill a great florist shop, the enormous temple bells that serve as chandeliers, the gilded wooden elephants caparisoned with a blanket made from woven flowers. The Thai people have a genius for turning floral arrangements into living works of art."

"Better include the way they carve fruit and vegetables into exquisite shapes."

"The ice sculptures too."

"Did you fly on to Phuket?"

"No."

He was alerted all at once. "You don't sound like you had any fun at all. Phuket is a great attraction in that part of the world. Phangnga Bay is famous for its profusion of limestone peaks rising out of the milky green water. There are countless caves as well. I'm not sure how many James Bond movies have used the bay as a location. And who was your companion in all this luxury?"

Her green eyes went dark. "Someone I fell very fast out of love with."

"Ah…your lover!" Despite himself his voice took on a dark edge. He hated the idea of her with her doctor lover. Knew he had no right. "Are we allowed to use the D word?"

"What's the D word?" she near whispered.

His gaze pinned her. "As in doctor?"

"We went home early."

"Weren't enjoying yourselves?" he asked sardonically.

"I wasn't enjoying myself," she corrected. "May we get off the D word?"

"Certainly." He bit off what he wanted to say. He didn't want to cheapen the extraordinary bond he had formed with her. "I don't like the sound of the D word either."

"Neither do I."

He was baffled. "Forgive me, Laura, but why spend any time at all with a man who only offered you trouble?"

"Try because he wouldn't leave me alone."

"All right, you're still in love with him even if you can't see a future?" He had a sensation of extreme anger directed towards her doctor, who sounded very much like a control freak..

"I'm not so involved I didn't love being kissed by you," Laura freely admitted.

He whistled softly beneath his breath. "The lady admits it."

"I couldn't hide it," she said simply.

"But I'm not the only man in your life?" He kept his tone deliberately light.

"Unfortunately, no. Not at this point in time."

"Be that as it may, Laura, it's not going to stop me from kissing you again," he warned. "I'd say you're in need of lots of love and kisses."

"The right kind," she murmured.

He took his eye off the track to study her face, a frown between his strongly marked black brows. "What do you know about violence?" A terrible suspicion opened up, although she looked as inviolate as a white orchid.

So difficult to answer—particularly because she couldn't bear anything to jeopardise their blossoming relationship. "It's everywhere, isn't it? One only has to watch the television or read the papers."

"Personal violence, Laura," he said, his expression very serious.

"I don't understand?" She couldn't meet that piercing gaze. She hated to lie, but lies at this stage seemed to be her only protection.

"I think you do." There was a flicker of something like anger or deep disappointment in the dark depths of his eyes.

"Evan, you're exhausting me with your questions." She tried to change the subject. "That's it, really." What had happened to her during her short marriage was so demeaning she couldn't bring herself to tell him about it and remain outwardly calm. Even with Sarah she'd been reduced to tears.

"So we get off the subject?"

"Please. But I'm grateful for your concern."

The truth was the shame crippled her. How could she involve Evan in her personal dramas? The best thing she had ever done was leave Colin. The next thing, the all-important thing, was to get legally free of him.

It was amazing to see light aircraft dotting the plain surrounding Wunnamurra's huge silver hangar, with its logo emblazoned on the roof. Even then it was a long way from the airstrip to the main compound where inside vehicles of all kinds, four-wheel drives, buses, trucks, vans—were parked all over.

Laura looked about her with open curiosity and amazement. "This is like a private kingdom," she murmured. There were outbuildings on all sides, staff bungalows, and what looked like a huge hall. As yet the legendary Wunnamurra homestead hadn't come into sight. They had arrived in good time. The funeral was set for eleven a.m., allowing plenty of time for visitors to attend the wake afterwards at the homestead before flying or driving out in full daylight.

"Homestead coming up," Evan said. "It's very grand."

"Obviously the McQueens are doing well," Laura observed dryly. "This is a small settlement in itself."

"The Outback homestead is the equivalent of the Englishman's stately home to these people," Evan said. "The pioneering families were and had to be pretty extraordinary. Those days seem a very romantic period in our short history, but hardship danger and death were facts of everyday life. The McQueens are a major pioneering family. From all accounts the late Mrs Ruth McQueen worked very hard to keep the station going after she lost her husband, Ewan. She was apparently a wonderful horsewoman, though they said she tended to be a bit ruthless with her horses.''

"As she was with people?" Laura asked quietly, remembering what she'd been told. "Sarah sounded very upset, but underneath I thought I detected some measure of release. It would be very daunting having to contend with family antagonism."

"Especially from a woman who had reigned supreme. I don't know how close to the house we can get. I think they're expecting a few hundred people. More, by the look of it."

"Is it okay if I stick close to you?"

He laughed briefly. "Laura, I have no intention of letting you out of my sight."

The homestead loomed up on top of a rise in the near flat landscape. It was the bluest day imaginable, and the magnificent pristine white building, two-storeyed, with deep verandahs on both levels, was like a picture cut-out against the sapphire sky. Trees towered high to the sides of the house. In front a great sweep of green lawn, no doubt watered by bores, curved down to a jewelled creek that meandered through the home gardens.

Now that she was here, Laura felt overwhelmed. She had grown up in a very comfortable and gracious environment, she had married into a wealthy established family, but her friend Sarah's future in-laws were among the very seriously rich. She knew there had been a great deal of trauma in Sarah's life, but now it was over.

They parked alongside many other cars, under the trees— Evan, man-like, soon finding a gap. He took her hand as she stepped out of the vehicle. "You can't leave your hat behind, Laura," he warned. "There's no way you can stand out in the sun. Certainly not with that skin."

"What I have with me is scarcely appropriate," she said a little nervously. All she'd been able to do was remove the

bright flowers and ribbons from one of her straw hats and
substitute a border of navy camellia-type flowers she had
managed to buy in town.

Evan reached in for the offending hat. "You'd look beautiful in anything. Here, put it on."

"Back to big brother?"

"It's certainly safer," he told her dryly, thinking the wide-
brimmed hat, dipping gently to one side, only set off her
natural beauty.

In whatever direction Laura looked there were people, but
the route to the McQueen family cemetery was orderly and
planned, with signs to show the way. Despite that, Laura was
glad Evan was with her. The place looked so vast she felt if
she stepped off the path she'd be lost for ever.

"We won't rush," Evan said, slowing her with a hand to
her elbow. "Plenty of time. I guess even Ruth McQueen
won't be in a hurry to get buried."

"I only hope I can get through this without tears," Laura
confessed, feeling her own emotions. "The last funeral I attended was my father's."

The family cemetery that held the graves of generations of
McQueens was reached through massive wrought-iron gates,
the black relieved by some splendid gilding. A large number
of mourners had already gathered, and the churchman in at-
tendance looked very dignified in his vestments.

Low borders of some dark green shrub flanked the path-
ways, trimmed to perfection. Around the perimeter of the
cemetery ran a high black wrought-iron fence.

Laura wondered what Sarah was thinking and feeling.

She could see the golden-haired Sarah standing beside her
splendid fiancé Kyall. Kyall was now head of the family. His
mother and father stood quietly to one side, a young girl at
Max Reardon's shoulder. That would be Kyall's young
cousin, brought home from her boarding school in Sydney.

Laura knew the dynastic name McQueen had overridden
Kyall's father's surname, Reardon. He had been christened
Kyall Readon-McQueen, but Laura had learned that over the

years the Reardon had simply disappeared. Laura wondered what Kyall's father thought about that. No doubt when Mrs McQueen had been alive her will had held sway.

A few feet away from her parents, almost as though she wished to stand alone, was a tall, but immensely graceful, very beautiful young woman who looked so much like Kyall that Laura realized immediately it had to be his sister, Christine. Black suit. Black hat. Black shoes. Perfect in every detail.

Over recent years Laura had seen that beautiful face and lean elegant body in many a glossy magazine, never imagining one day she would be looking directly at the international model.

About twenty feet away from her the Claydon family stood respectfully. The Claydons were another influential pioneering family. She had heard mention of Mitchell Claydon, a childhood friend of Sarah's, but this was the first time she'd laid eyes on him. A Robert Redford look-alike. His blond head, as golden as Sarah's, was uncovered to the sun. He was appropriately dressed in a dark suit, his hands folded quietly in front of him, but he gave off an aura of intensity more than calmness.

She caught the blue blaze of his eyes. It was unmistakable who he was staring at. Christine Reardon. She remembered Sarah telling her Christine and Mitchell Claydon had been as close at one time as she and Kyall.

So what had happened? Mitchell Claydon cut a very dashing figure, even in his formal funeral clothes. Judging from his expression he hadn't forgotten Christine either.

Finally all the mourners grouped themselves around the family plot. The pall bearers appeared. Laura stared off into the middle distance.

''You all right?'' Evan bent his dark head over her, grasping her hand.

She didn't know what to say. I am when I'm with you. Fancy burdening him with that! She felt wonderfully secure in his company, but not as a big brother. She couldn't begin to explain herself, or what she was allowing to happen. She was still imprisoned in her marriage, yet when she was in Evan's arms she threw all reservations to the winds.

No good the subterfuge. But emotion mocked at reason. Laura did all she could do. She nodded.

CHAPTER NINE

NOT all that long after the death of Ruth McQueen the town was rocked by an even greater shock. To the town's bolt upright astonishment came the dramatic revelation that Sarah Dempsey, resident doctor, had given birth to a child at the tender age of fifteen.

Sarah! The town could scarcely take it in. Everyone offered an opinion. No one condemned. Sarah was their doctor, a good one, born and bred in the town. She was one of them.

The father of Sarah's baby was her present fiancé, Kyall McQueen, universally admired and a very handsome, egalitarian guy for all his family's wealth. The great question was, How had everyone missed it? Ruby Hall, the chief spreader of gossip, had ears like a stethoscope. She could detect the slightest murmur. She had even been known to press her ears to walls. Yet Ruby had noticed nothing. In the midst of their shock, the people of the bush town enjoyed a guffaw at Ruby's expense.

Once the story broke it swept around the town like brush fire, embellished with every telling. Betty Dawson, who was old enough to know better, told her circle of friends she'd heard twins, but no one was left in any doubt that a terrible mishap had occurred in the small private maternity hospital on the east coast where Sarah had been taken—or banished, and a quick guess-around blamed Kyall's grandmother—to have her child. A daughter.

Tragedy had befallen young Sarah. She had been told her baby had died. Wicked negligence on the hospital's part. The hospital had been torn down to make way for a service station; it should have been sued. Apparently Sarah's baby had somehow been swapped with another infant girl, born at the same time. That baby *had* died. Sarah's baby had gone home with the wrong mother. No questions had been asked.

"Bloody odd!" mumbled the town publican to the bar, full of sympathy for the beautiful Sarah, a favourite of his.

The upshot was that the young Sarah had been left to live with the heartbreak. The father, Kyall McQueen, then barely sixteen, heir to Wunnamurra Station and the apple of his powerful grandmother's eye, had never been told of Sarah's pregnancy.

Why not? Of course it had been the grandmother. It had to be, considering she had frowned on the friendship. Everyone agreed Ruth McQueen had been one scary lady. Undoubtedly there was a story. Not that they were likely to hear it. Powerful families like the McQueens kept a tight lid on their affairs.

In the old days, when Sarah and Kyall had been youngsters, everyone had thought their extraordinary relationship right through childhood to adolescence romantic. That had been the general view, their youth and beauty sparking nostalgia. Everyone had known nothing could come of it. Too big a social gap. The McQueens were Outback royalty and Ruth McQueen had lived right up to her reputation as the world's worst snob. Sarah's father, a "good bloke", had been a shearer in Wunnamurra's sheds. The mother, "poor Muriel", as everyone called her after she lost her husband, had run the general store.

· So, the loss of her baby had plagued Sarah for the rest of her life. As well it might. And now the whole town offered solidarity—not only because Sarah was their resident doctor and the McQueens practically owned the town, but because this was a genuine love story. It was beginning to take on epic proportions. Everyone was expecting a fairy tale wedding, maybe a public holiday. The McQueens had funded many a celebration in the town...

The true sensation was that Sarah and Kyall had discovered proof their child had not died. Incredibly they had found her—healthy, living, beautiful—holidaying with a schoolfriend on a station some hundred miles west of Koomera Crossing. After all the years of agony fate had found its conscience and handed Sarah and Kyall a well-deserved miracle from heaven. For weeks on end the town was to talk of nothing else.

"I suppose my story will become part of Koomera Crossing folklore," Sarah said wryly one day, finding it very hard these days to keep back the emotional tears. She looked for support to Laura and Harriet, who were eyeing her with great empathy. All three were sitting around Harriet's kitchen table, drinking coffee and nibbling at the delicious little confections Harriet had whipped up for them.

"After so much pain, so much tragedy, a miracle!" Laura said, blessing Sarah's courageous heart.

"If anyone deserves a little happiness in life it's Sarah," Harriet asserted, her near sternness covering a flurry of her own emotion.

Harriet, as the long-time head of the school—a period of thirty years—was a real institution in the town. Now in her late sixties, but looking nowhere near it, she was highly regarded, even revered. Sarah loved her old mentor. Laura could see why. Evan too had grown fond of her, calling Harriet "Aunty Mame", with a gentle, mocking smile. Harriet was a woman of culture, much travelled to exotic places, and a startlingly unconventional dresser, with a style all her own, rather plain of face but with fine all-seeing grey eyes and a rich, resonant voice.

"So, I'm to be a mother, my friends," Sarah announced with a heartbreaking smile. "A mother and a wife. Kyall wanted us to settle down and have a family. We have a family now, our beautiful Fiona. I can't wait for you to meet her. We're to be married as soon as possible, after a little bow to tradition. I couldn't ever begin to like or respect Ruth McQueen and I wouldn't want to meet a woman like her again in my lifetime, but she will never cease to be Kyall's grandmother. If she cared for no one else, she adored him."

"They should have saved that for her epitaph," Harriet remarked crisply. "'Here lies Ruth McQueen, matriarch of the McQueen clan. She cared for only one human being in her entire life.'" Harriet reached out to pat Sarah's hands.

Ruth McQueen, wicked woman that she was, had finally gone.

Out on the pavement in front of Harriet's rather grand colonial, which was furnished with all sorts of finds from her travels, including two eight-feet-high Maori totem poles flanking her front door, Harriet held Laura to her promise to come to dinner the following Saturday evening.

"Evan's coming." Harriet beamed in Laura's direction. "I hear you two have struck up a nice friendship."

Laura, fully aware that Sarah had confided a little of her circumstances to her great friend, answered fervently. "After a husband who couldn't say one civil word to me Evan's gallantry has been like a healing balm."

"You haven't spoken about Colin yet?" Sarah took a quick glance at her watch. She had to get back to the hospital, but she had appreciated the break and the comfort of her friends.

"I will—I will."

"You should do, my dear," Harriet suggested quietly. "What is it you fear most?"

"The loss of Evan's esteem," Laura said without hesitation. "His respect. I've come to value his friendship so much."

"Why should he respect you less?" Harriet countered, studying the lovely young woman in front of her. If golden-haired Sarah looked like an angel this one looked like the heroine of a romance. How could any man bear to hurt such a gentle young woman?

"Because it would appear I had no respect for myself, Harriet. I can't blot out the life I led."

"Oh, Laura, you were a victim." Sarah had tried hard to impress this on her friend but it took some doing. She gave Laura a quick hug. "You were a young woman overwhelmed by a violent husband. A man you thought you loved."

Harriet's grey eyes sparkled with outrage. "Good God!"

"It should have been different," Laura said. "*I* should have been different. Stronger. I can't tell Evan yet. I know you'll keep my confidence."

"Be sure of it, my dear. But I don't think it's going to take all that much longer for you to develop such trust in Evan you'll be able to confide in him too. You think your husband will be looking for you?"

"He will be looking for me, Harriet. You can count on that. Every day I experience some moments of panic, but I'm gradually getting them under control. Knowing Colin, I won't be surprised to find him at my door one day."

"You've got friends, Laura," Sarah said. "You're nowhere near as vulnerable as you suppose. Now, I must fly. Morris has held the fort long enough." Sarah turned to kiss Harriet and then Laura in turn. "Kyall will be in Adelaide on business for a week, so he won't be at the dinner party, but Morris will."

"I'm looking forward to meeting him." Laura smiled, knowing Morris Hughes was Sarah's offsider at the hospital and Harriet's special friend. "Could be a romance on the wind!"

"That's all settled, then," Harriet said with satisfaction, graciously closing Sarah's door as she slid behind the driver's seat. "I'm sure it's going to be a lovely evening. I've already planned the menu."

When Laura arrived home Evan was on the driveway, unloading his car. She approached slowly. The cottage had no garage the owners apparently had parked on the grassy allotment to the rear of the cottage, but Evan in the space of an afternoon had put up a car port for her on his own large block.

She waved hello, feeling her skin start to tingle. Some people knew real, true love—marital bliss. It hadn't been for her. Now this. She was still tied to Colin and falling in love with Evan, which made the situation all the worse. And she *was* falling in love with this big, powerful, dark-haired man, leaning back against his four-wheel drive watching her drive in. He knew she had secrets. What he didn't know was how monstrous they were.

She parked and he came alongside. "What have you been up to?" He bent to look in at her.

"Coffee break with Sarah and Harriet at Harriet's amazing house. All those artefacts!"

"Harriet is very different." He smiled, standing back while she got out of her car.

"I can see why you like her. You're very different too." She smiled up at him as her longings grew.

"It's okay to be different, Laura," he said. "I'm glad you're here. I have something for you."

"Really?" Instantly she was intrigued. What would she do when he went out of her life? She was too needy. Wasn't the speed with which she had fallen in love with him proof of that?

"Come along." He stared down at her for a minute. She was standing very still, with an odd, pensive expression on her face. Her skin, even in the harsh sunlight, was flawless, baby-smooth, poreless. Her hair flowed down her back.

"I've still got some of those home-grown vegetables you brought me," she told him, thinking it was market day and he'd perhaps stocked up.

"Not vegetables," he said, moving back to his vehicle.

"They were lovely."

"Good. You look very lovely today," he remarked lightly, nearly laughing aloud at the understatement.

"Thank you." She glanced down at herself. "It's probably this dress."

It occurred to him not for the first time that she was remarkably free of vanity.

"What is it?" she asked, her eyes very bright.

"You'll see. It's living, breathing…"

Her lips parted and she blushed. "Now you've got me. What is it, Evan?"

"Turn around."

"Okay." She obeyed. "Do I have to close my eyes?"

"You can if you want to."

She did, almost feeling like a child again, with life full of beauty and love.

"You can look now." She turned while he lifted the lid of a basket. There, lying on a fragment of blanket, was a bundle of black fur with eyes of jade.

"A kitten!" she cried out in delighted astonishment.

"You told me once you loved cats."

"Doesn't everyone?"

"No." he said, very dryly.

"Isn't she beautiful?" Laura started to put her hand out.

"He."

"Oh! Can I hold him?"

Her lovely face had lit up so much it was almost unbearable not to sweep her into his arms. Intuition told him he couldn't go too fast. "Why not? He's yours. That's if you want him."

"He's really mine?"

Her smile was so sweet, so grateful. "You're great to give a present to."

She gazed off into the distance, over the incredible sweeping vistas she loved about the town.

Perplexed, he watched her. "What is it? What's the matter?"

"Nothing, just a funny moment."

Colin, furious, shouting. *"Come here and say thank you. You can't appreciate anything."*

"I wish to God you'd tell me."

How she understood his frustration. "I'm perfectly all right, Evan." She looked down at the little kitten. "Oh, you darling little thing!" she crooned. "Aren't you adorable? And so soft!"

"I knew I had to get him for you the minute I saw the iridescent green eyes."

"You're always thinking of something for me," she said gratefully, tilting her head to look up at him.

"You need kindness, that's why."

"Would you buy anyone a kitten?" she asked, a little crestfallen.

"No, I wouldn't. I bought the kitten for you."

"Well, I love it." She flashed him a joyful smile. "But

what will I do with it if I have to go back?'' She couldn't bear to think about leaving the security of the town, her new friends, Evan.

''Back where?'' he asked, the dark brooding returned to his eyes.

''Back to my old life.''

''You want to make a go of it with your doctor?''

''I need to resolve it,'' she said, imagining how very, very difficult that was going to be.

''So how long do you think it's going to take?'' He'd soon found he wasn't immune to jealousy.

''I ask myself that every day.''

''Brave, beautiful Laura!''

''I wish!'' Yet she smiled, a hint of triumph in it. Life was a journey. It was how one handled it in the tough times that counted.

''Ah, well, we'll see.'' Evan said, never guessing the full extent of the damage Laura had suffered behind closed doors. ''Now, I've got everything else you'll need,'' he added, indicating the full basket. ''You keep the basket. Puss will probably sleep in it, it's so comfortable.'' His hand moved over hers to stroke the kitten, coming into contact with hers. He didn't disguise the pleasure.

A force like a whirlwind rushed through Laura. His hand on her skin. He knew how to kiss, how to touch, how to look at her with his dark eyes. There was just no one like him. She was starting to feel quite light-headed, as though she was floating.

''Why don't we get you and your kitten home?'' he suggested. ''What are we going to call him?''

''Something musical? Freddy—short for Freddy Chopin?'' she suggested playfully. ''Wolfgang's a bit much.'' She was carrying too much emotion inside her. It was riding high right up to her throat. ''Harriet and I think you look a bit like Beethoven.''

''What?'' He grimaced wryly. ''Behind Harriet's acerbic exterior lies a romantic. I don't mind Freddy for the kitten as he belongs to a musician.''

"Then Freddy he is. Look, Evan, he loves me already."
In fact the kitten was purring ecstatically, snuggling up
against her breast.

"Lord, who wouldn't?" Evan replied, too softly to be
heard. He bestowed on her what he hoped was an indulgent
smile when he wanted to wrap her and the kitten in his arms.

"I think this is the nicest thing that has ever happened to
me since I was a child."

He laughed shortly. "Surely your doctor showers you with
gifts?"

Her stroking hand on the kitten paused. "He does, but I've
never loved anything so much as this. Thank you, Evan."
She kept her head bent so he wouldn't see the expression in
her eyes.

"It'll be company for you." His tone lightened. "Cats are
highly intelligent. It won't be long before it's well trained."

Her smile came out again. "There you are, Freddy. When
you're properly trained you can sleep on my bed."

It seemed to Evan there could be no better place.

CHAPTER TEN

THEY walked together to Harriet's house. Laura loved this time of evening, when the stars started to come out in all their desert glory. It was a phenomenal display, far exceeding any she had seen over the costal cities. And every bright star in the sky had an aboriginal myth to account for its origin. She loved reading about them, and seeing the extraordinary aboriginal art proudly displayed in the Shire Hall

The Southern Cross followed them as they walked, its outline brilliantly defined in the soft purple sky. Its points were the spirits of the aboriginal ancestors. The diamond-encrusted river that curved across the sky was the Milky Way, its billions of twinkling stars the camp fires of the ancestors who had flown up there as a reward for the good lives they had led. The Evening Star, hanging by its long stalk, was a lotus, living in the Dreaming Country of the moon.

The aboriginal symbol for a star was a lotus, she had learned. She had admired those paintings—the flower the star's bright glow, the stalk the star's path through the night sky. And there was Orion, the mighty hunter with his jeweled belt. The constellation Scorpio, lovers who had broken tribal law, and the lesser stars of the constellation the boomerang and throwing sticks that had been hurled after them.

"You're quiet," Evan said, tucking her arm more firmly beneath his.

"I'm marvelling at the brilliance of the stars. Thinking about the aboriginal myths. The Dreaming hadn't come alive for me until I made the journey out here to Koomera Crossing. Now I find myself making a study of aboriginal beliefs as set out in the myths and legends. They're wonderfully dramatic."

"They are. They involve great Beings and amazing geological events which do contain the essence of truth. It's quite extraordinary—we have an ancient people whose traditions and cultures have scarcely changed in tens of thousands of years. You'll understand more fully what the land means to the aboriginal people when we visit the Red Centre.''

"I can't wait," she said, looking up at him with a smile.

"Neither can I, for that matter. As far as I'm concerned no other region in the world can equal its stark primeval beauty. The Timeless Land, the oldest part of the earth's crust. You're going to love it.''

"A real adventure." Her voice was full of pleasure. "I love this town too, with all its quaint little workers' cottages and grander colonials, like yours and Harriet's. The mix of modest and grandeur, the latticed Queenlanders, with their broad wraparound verandahs to protect the house from the sun. Some of the houses are almost submerged in greenery. It's odd on the desert fringe.''

"Courtesy bore water from the Great Artesian Basin," he explained. "It lies below a large part of the Queensland Outback, providing invaluable supplies of water, as you can imagine.''

"I've just realized I'm hungry," she said as they walked up Harriet's front path, catching the drift of succulent aromas.

"That's good, because Harriet's a splendid cook.''

The exterior lights and the lights from the house lit up their way. Nearing the steps, Evan took her hand again.

"Watch those high heels." He glanced down at her pretty pink slingbacks.

"I like to look taller," Laura responded a little breathlessly, feeling her heart racing with excitement every time he touched her.

"You look very beautiful.''

How his deep voice stirred her, as if her heart was a cello string. "That's the second time you've told me.''

"I was hoping you'd give me a smile.''

"Didn't I smile the first time? I'd be astonished if I hadn't.''

"As a matter of fact you didn't." Their glances briefly

locked. "You looked very much like your thoughts were elsewhere."

He was far too perceptive. She'd been reminded inevitably of other times. Colin introducing her so proudly to new people. "My beautiful wife." The sheer lunacy of it. She wondered if she'd have faired better had she been plain, not the "classic chocolate box", as he'd often labelled her with heavy ridicule.

"I heard you all the same," she assured Evan quietly.

"Good." He couldn't help the fact it sounded clipped.

Harriet must have heard their voices, because she hurried out onto the porch, giving Laura a quick hug. "Don't you look lovely!" she said warmly. "Such a pretty dress. Evan, I'm so pleased you could come."

"You're too good a cook, Harriet," Evan said, bending his dark head to peck Harriet's cheek.

"I don't know if you've heard about my idea—Kyall's, really—of opening a restaurant in the town, but you will," Harriet said enthusiastically.

"Wouldn't teaching be easier?" Evan asked, thinking running a restaurant would be hard work. Harriet was well into her sixties.

"I don't doubt it, but I feel like a new challenge. In fact I'm very excited at the prospect."

"Good for you. Count on me as a patron. I suspect Laura too."

"I *am* counting on it." Harriet laughed. "Now, come in and meet the rest of my guests, Laura. Evan knows them, of course. And Sarah's here."

"Lovely!" Laura felt very peaceful with her friend Sarah around.

Harriet was in high spirits. Tonight she wore a fantastic flowing garment of vibrant, swirling colours Laura thought might have been put on backwards—whether by design or accident, she wasn't sure.

Harriet leaned closer, speaking directly to Laura. "Darling, if you think I've got this on backwards, you're right. I thought it made it look better."

"You look gorgeous, Harriet. I should have brought my camera."

Harriet beamed at her. "Caftans are back in. I read that in Paris *Vogue*. I bought the material for this one in Morocco. Ran it up myself. Made a reasonable job of it, I think."

"Harriet is multi-talented." A smile of warm amusement appeared on Evan's face. "You have yet to hear her playing her viola."

"I'd love that."

"This man plays the cello like I imagine the Archangel Gabriel might." Harriet lifted her head, looking up at Evan with obvious pleasure. "The big, full tone. No question it's a man playing. I think our Evan here has seen a great deal of life," she challenged, her grey gaze growing pointed. "It's all in his playing. It creates real electricity in the listener. You're looking wonderfully relaxed tonight, Evan. That sharp, passionate mind seems soothed."

"You think so?" Evan asked dryly.

"At least you're not so fiercely private."

"That's because, my dear Harriet, I acknowledge you as a friend," he told her suavely.

And what of Laura? Harriet thought, thoroughly intrigued by this developing situation. The way Laura and Evan moved together, their whole body language, suggested a certain degree of intimacy, of understanding. But lovely Laura, in her summery dusky pink dress, light as air, was still married to her dreadful husband. Laura would have to tell Evan before they became more deeply involved. If they hadn't reached that point already...

"Heavens, you're not going to stay out there all night?" They heard Sarah call from the front room.

"Coming, dear." With a burst of rich laughter, Harriet swept her guests into the house.

The evening was destined to be a great success. Eight people sat down to dinner: Harriet at one end of the beautifully appointed table, her "friend" Dr Morris Hughes, Sarah's colleague at the hospital, at the other, Laura and Evan opposite each other, Sarah beside Evan, Laura beside Alex Matheson, a very elegant dark-haired, grey-eyed man in his early thirties, the conductor of the town's orchestra, and a very pleasant middle-aged couple, the Wards—Selma and Alan—who were right at the top of Harriet's network of friends, made up the numbers.

Selma, it transpired, was Harriet's "second cook", and was very good and very interested in Harriet's new venture.

Harriet certainly lived up to her reputation as having special culinary talents, Laura thought as the conversation eddied around her. Apparently Harriet's dinner parties featured a variety of cuisines: Malay, Thai, Indian, Japanese, Chinese and occasionally classic French. But she was a great champion of the more exotic cuisines.

Tonight was Thai. Khao Soi Gai—egg noddles with a spicy chicken curry—to start, followed by sautéed beef tenderloin with black pepper sauce and green baby vegetables, then a choice of mango cheesecake on a pistachio sponge base or iced banana parfait with coconut crust for those who had room for dessert.

They all did.

Laura by this point felt all her tensions and tortured thoughts of Colin had fallen away. Introductions had gone well for her. All the guests were warm, friendly people who'd accepted her immediately. The talk had ranged over a wide number of interesting and entertaining topics. Harriet and Evan, who appeared to have really come out of his shell, had tossed them up as if they were throwing up juggling balls. Alex Matheson, whose elegant manner appeared undampened by the fact he suffered periodic bouts of near blindness, had paid special attention to the fact Laura was a Conservatorium-trained pianist.

That at least she had been able to admit, though she couldn't help noticing with relief no one delved too deeply into her background. An unspoken agreement? Whatever it was, she was grateful.

The Wards were members of the orchestra too, Alex told her. Alan on clarinet; Selma on flute. Obviously the love of music ran through them all, forming an immediate bond. Their music-making was a source of considerable pleasure and satisfaction, not only to them but to the people of the town.

"When do we hear *you* play?" Alex asked Laura. One would never have known he suffered from a very serious eye problem by looking at him. His grey eyes were crystal-clear.

"I promise you you'll enjoy it." Evan glanced across at his friend. "Laura's fingers simply draw the music from the keys."

"As do yours from the strings," Alex said graciously. "Evan's the rock on which the rest of the group rests," he confided to Laura. "I don't suppose you'd consider joining us in a quintet for piano and strings? I'm useless these days as a pianist."

"Not true." Very firmly said from the rest of the table.

"Well, not what I was." Alex shrugged. "We've only just started working on Beethoven's *Ghost*. Evan can tell you. We're going to rehearse from now on at his house, so you wouldn't have to go far."

"I'd be honoured," Laura said, allowing her eyes to touch on Evan across the gleaming expanse of the table: snowy linen and lace tablemats, sumptuous oriental china and dishes, crystal wine glasses, a long low arrangement of white butterfly orchids that trembled in the breeze.

He was a very striking-looking man, with his strong distinctive features, the breadth of his shoulders emphasized by his soft beige jacket with cotton dress shirt beneath. She knew there was a lot of turbulence and intensity in him, but tonight he had concentrated on being witty and charming.

"Marvellous!"

"I beg your pardon?" Abruptly, Laura realized in staring at Evan she hadn't heard what Alex had just said to her.

"I said marvellous that you'll join us," Alex repeated, not missing a thing. Smoothly he saluted her with his wine glass. "Welcome on board, Laura."

"That went extremely well," Evan remarked as they made their way home. Knowing Harriet always served her guests wine, they had walked the easy strolling distance to Harriet's house rather than take Evan's car.

"I enjoyed every minute. I thought you and Harriet made a great team. Both of you so witty and clever. You've been to so many places! And I didn't know Harriet was a flirt!" She laughed.

"He's a very nice man, and he so enjoys Harriet. Sarah had a lovely time too, but she's missing Kyall."

"They'll be married soon and they'll have their daughter," Evan said quietly.

"Like a miracle, isn't it?"

"Thank God they do happen. But no miracles for Alex, I'm afraid."

"What exactly is wrong with his eyesight? His eyes are perfectly clear."

"They were tonight. Other times—the bad times—they look quite different. Whatever it is and I don't fully understand the condition, it's quite rare."

"With no cure?" Laura's voice conveyed her sympathy.

"Maybe I'm entirely wrong, but I think some of Alex's problem could be psychological. He's highly strung, as my mother used to say, and as close-lipped about his past as we are. All three of us could be classed as damaged people."

"Something should be done to help him."

"Something should be done to help all of us," Evan said wryly. "Do you think you'll ever be happily married, Laura?"

She had her opening. Shouldn't she seize it? Tell him at the end of this lovely evening: I'm married, Evan. Not only that, but married to an abusive man, terrible as it is. She hesitated fatally, thinking how desolate she would feel if he dropped her hand like a hot cake.

The moment went by. "Look at you," she evaded, summoning up a light tone. "Why aren't *you* thinking of marriage? I've deduced you haven't led a normal life, but don't you want a wife, a family?"

"Everything in good time."

"That's not an answer."

"All right, Laura, would you marry me?"

For a minute she couldn't move on. She froze, shocked out of an answer until she realized his tone had been sardonic.

"I couldn't," she said finally, and released her breath.

"Of course you couldn't. You're in love with your doctor."

"No, I'm not." Sadness mingled with utter truth.

"You just like being under his thumb?" He regretted it the instant he'd said it. Not that he didn't mean it but it had sounded chastening.

She flushed. "We've had such a lovely night. Don't let's spoil it." She couldn't bear that, not when she was experiencing such peace it was like a dream.

"How are those heels taking the walk?" he asked, immediately reacting to her tone and changing subjects.

"Fine. I'm used to them."

Being with him in this glorious star-filled night was rapture. She hadn't needed three glasses of beautiful white wine over dinner to intoxicate her blood. She was travelling on a magic carpet. Just the two of them in the quiet tree-shrouded street with the heavens over them ablaze.

He paused at her front gate. "I'll see you in."

She didn't say no. No matter how far she tried to remove herself from thoughts of Colin there was always the threat of his materialising out of the darkness one day.

"Would you like to come in for a moment?" she found herself murmuring. "I left Freddy in his basket."

"Just for a moment." He felt a sudden sharp ache for his own aloneness. "I'll check the house for you."

"Why? What do you think you'll discover?"

"What you're so damned worried about." He took the key out of her nerveless hand, inserted it in the lock and opened the cottage door. He found the switch, flooding the hallways with soft golden light. As he turned his head, he registered her expression.

She stood there, staring back at him, lips parted. Petite, delicate in her pink dress, her dark gleaming hair framing her face. He wanted to take that lovely face into his hands. He wanted to kiss the soft, tender curves of her mouth. He wanted to chase the shadows from her jewelled eyes.

He knew he only had to touch her and the want would turn into a burning fever. Her pretty dress clung to her slender body, the low V neckline, delicately ruffled, drawing his eyes to the exquisite contours of her breasts. For an instant he allowed himself to see her arched against him. He knew there was passion in her. He had heard it in her music.

"Evan?" She too was conscious they were poised on a knife-edge.

"Things to do." He moved abruptly into the parlour, turning on the lights. At first he didn't notice the kitten staring up at him. It was so small, so black, a bundle of fur almost undetectable except for the brilliant colour of its eyes. "Freddy's awake," he called over his shoulder. "Probably wants some milk and some company."

"Oh, sweetheart!" Laura followed Evan into the room, bending to pick up her kitten. "I bet you've been missing me."

Evan didn't speak, but watched them for a moment. He'd known a number of beautiful women in his life. He'd imagined himself in love with the traitor Monika. But this young woman had become painfully important to him in much too short a space of time. In a sense it was difficult to understand how profoundly she'd affected him. She was beautiful, certainly, and intelligent, gifted. Her laughter was lovely. Her smile. Was it her delicate femininity that made him think she needed protection? If she had a problem with her doctor lover, as she must have to flee him, she was clearly unwilling to give up the relationship.

He knew from the first moment he saw her she was going to affect his life. What made him think it would be for the good? If he allowed himself to fall in love with her—hell, he *was* in love with her—she could only cause him pain. Surely he'd had enough experience of pain to guard himself from it? And living his kind of life—if he returned to it—he had to keep himself free.

Nonetheless, he allowed himself to be beguiled by the sight of young woman and kitten. She could have posed for one of those enchantingly sentimental Victorian paintings. Yet she was a woman of mystery. This whole damned thing with her doctor lover was baffling. Unresolved. Obviously the man saw her as a trophy, an appendage. The thought upset him.

He heard her cooing to her bundle of fluff as it tenderly nuzzled her neck before she carried the kitten into the kitchen—no doubt for a warm drink of milk. It had grown in a matter of days. Clearly she loved it. For such a small gesture on his part it gave him immense pleasure.

The cottage was empty, so he took a minute to check the detached laundry. Really, she couldn't be safer in this town. There was no crime. Nothing beyond kids getting up to pranks or the occasional teenager somehow getting hold of enough alcohol to make them drunk. They certainly wouldn't be served at the pub, where every last kid was known right down to the year of birth. He glanced around the laundry, then walked the short distance to the back door. He didn't know if she'd unlocked it but tapped on it all the same.

"Evan?"

Even through the solid timber door he could hear the quaver in her voice.

"Yes. Hope I didn't frighten you?" he called. What the hell was this? God, he was six-four and he had a black belt. He'd be good at protecting her from whatever it was that made her feel especially vulnerable.

When he stepped inside the cottage she was shaking. "I was checking the laundry," he explained, staring down at her. "I thought you'd realize I'd check around."

"Of course." She turned away, but not before he saw her face.

Perturbed, he turned her around again, his hands firm on her shoulders. "Laura, what is this? You think I don't know fear when I see it? I've witnessed it many times in life. If you feel like this, you must tell someone. Tell *me*. Who's going to come to your door?"

"I'm so sorry, Evan. I'm just a nervous woman," she

apologized. "Some women are. We're not all brave, especially when someone knows you're on your own." She was horrified that she continually failed the test to confide in him when she kept promising herself she would.

"You're not on your own, Laura," he protested. "Is this man of yours so damn bad you're frightened he's going to come after you? What then? He can't force you to do anything you don't want. Has he some hold over you? Is he somehow blackmailing you? Has he made you do things you didn't like? What is it? Has he been making threats? Saying he'll attempt suicide if you leave him? Is he saying any goddamn thing to hold onto you?" he asked tautly.

She bit back a moan. Colin had done all those things. "All this because you gave me a fright?"

"You don't dare tell me, do you?"

The truth, the whole truth and nothing but the truth. Those few moments of involuntary fright bore witness to the unhealed scars Colin had left on her. Her beautiful eyes suddenly brimmed with tears. There was such shame deep within her for the ugly secret she carried around with her. It hit at her soul and all but undermined her self-respect.

"Don't cry, Laura," he begged. God help him she broke his heart.

"Oh, Evan!" She began to flail his chest helplessly.

"Come here to me." She might have been a kitten in his arms, all softness and delicate bones.

The instant his arms closed around her she felt less frantic. Regaining a measure of control. This was Evan, not the monster she'd married. She pressed her body against his, feeding on his abundant strength. She loved the smell that came off his skin: like incense, warm, clean, male, already familiar to her as someone very dear. She had the sensation she was melting into him, hungry for the tenderness of the hand that stroked her. Such moments were idyllic. With Evan there would be no loss of control, no rush to violence.

"You're not going to go to sleep on me again, are you? This happens every time I hold you in my arms." His voice sounded indulgent, though a passionate desire for her was stirring his flesh.

"I may do," she murmured, wanting these moments to last.

"You haven't been treated properly, have you, Laura?"

"*You* treat me properly, Evan."

"You know I want to make love to you?"

"Yes." She trembled, overcome by the desire that rose at his call.

"Can you handle it?" He tipped up her head, to hold her green gaze.

"I don't know that I'm any good at making love," she confessed.

"Aren't you?" His voice was both tender. "You could have fooled me. You need to feel safe, Laura. That's all it is. You'll be safe with me. We'll go slowly. If you become frightened, we'll draw back. You're holding your breath. Let it go. I've kissed you before."

"I loved it."

"You'll have your chance to prove it." He swung her up into his arms, carrying her through to the parlour, where he held her cradled on the sofa.

He was so much in love with this strange contradictory girl he felt the force of it rise like the great jet of a fountain. Nonetheless he began to kiss her, his passionate desire almost overcoming his promise to go slowly. She was afraid of hurt. He couldn't possibly risk hurting her with his vastly superior strength or the fiery energy that was in him.

Her mouth was so sweet, blissful, the velvet inside, her tongue. Her arousal was apparent. He could hear it in the soft little gathering cries that increased his own urgency.

He stroked the silky length of her arms, drew her up so she was even closer. Body to body. She clung to him, but he could sense a kind of conflict was happening inside her body, inside her head.

"Do you want me to stop?" He feared he was already too far along.

"No!" Her whisper was fervent. "It's not you, it's me. You're wonderful."

"So are you. Surely you know that?"

How could she answer? Tell him how Colin had habitually demeaned her? "Make love to me, Evan."

He felt his senses reel. "You know I might reach a point when I won't be able to stop? Even for you." He had to warn her.

"You might discover you don't want me." That was dredged up from the taunts of the past.

"That's not going to happen, Laura. Trust me."

She sighed as if she were unburdening herself of all fears and anxieties. "All I want is for you to love me."

Love her he did! He made her whole body bloom, her white skin turning roseate with the heat of her blood. She lay on her bed, her hair spread around her body, naked except for the cool white sheet, while Evan turned her to face him. He kissed her face, her ears, her throat and her breasts, moved his mouth over her stomach, moving lower and lower, very quiet about it, while her body clenched and unclenched as only rapture followed the thrilling trail of fire.

The most wonderful thing was happening to her. Up until then marital sex had been a nightmare. This flowering, this warm languor, was exquisite, though her breath came shorter and sharper as the life force flowed through her.

He was speaking very gently. She couldn't speak herself. She was lost in the multitude of sensations his mouth and hands were calling forth with absolute quiet mastery.

Starlight showered the room; little squares of radiant moonlight fell on the rug. She knew he was propped up on an elbow, looking down at her face. She couldn't see him now. Her eyes had closed tightly as the shimmering rapture mounted. She had to hold it in. Treasure it. She'd endured so much suffering.

He was tracing the contours of her breasts, his hands so strong yet so exquisitely tender as they circled towards the tightly furled nipple. She was blind. Blind to everything but pleasure. She had dreaded night-time, going to bed, the object of Colin's sick obsession. She had never experienced anything remotely like this, her body shuddering not with pain but with a sensuality so voluptuous it was consuming her. There was no assault. This had nothing to do with bodily assault. This was the kind of lovemaking that approached pure magic.

"Laura?" He brushed his lips against hers. "Look at me."

Even though she was drifting on a great wave of sexual excitement she heard his call. He kissed her naked shoulder, looked into her open eyes. "You're exquisite! So exquisite you move me to tears."

Imagine that! He thought her exquisite! How glorious those words sounded after Colin's destructive names.

"You're ready for me, aren't you?"

Such tenderness she had never known.

Her breath exhaled on a "Yes!" She had discovered the purest kind of desire. Now all she needed to make it perfect was their union.

Slowly, slowly, he entered her, holding down all momentum. He felt the fluttering in her womb, then the strong contraction to enclose him. Agony for him and yet an extravagant radiating pleasure. He wanted desperately to be gentle with her, but he didn't know how to contain the deep driving male urge that might hurl him over the edge. Love was a flame!

He bore down, waited, heard her utter little moans he deduced as pleasure. The moans stretched out into a sob of wanting...wanting... He couldn't mistake it. He began his plunge into her lovely receptive body, exultant as she met him with the most ravishing desire of her own.

Instantly he was empowered. He held back no longer. And his last thought before passion controlled him was that he could never lose her. This woman held his heart in her hands.

CHAPTER ELEVEN

THE period before Sarah's wedding marked the happiest time of Laura's life. The enormous sense of guilt which she'd associated with sex—she could never have called it love-making with Colin—had totally disappeared. Evan had given her such reassurance, such confidence in her capacity to give and receive pleasure, that her emotional boundaries had run out to the horizons.

She wasn't a woman caged. She was free. She was able to enjoy life, to eat, to sleep, to resume the music that was in her blood. She was able to interact with all the new friends she was making. She could see people liked her from their smiling, welcoming faces.

That soul-destroying sense of fear and hopelessness she had endured living with Colin she'd pushed into some other place and shut the door. There were times when she had the occasional breakthrough—a kind of panic attack induced by some particularly bitter memory of her husband. But her new life at Koomera Crossing was beginning to take shape. She was in the process of becoming strong.

Several hours of the day she had taken to doing voluntary work at the Bush Hospital—something that gained her much gratitude from Sarah and the staff.

Funding for rural and bush hospitals wasn't high—Koomera Crossing Bush Hospital couldn't do without regular injections of money from the McQueens, and the town itself staged fundraisers to help out. Laura, financially secure, insisted on taking no payment herself.

When she wasn't doing clerical work, helping to clear the workload, she offered her services to the patients who had been admitted—reading aloud to them, helping them write letters, simply chatting, using her own gentle, very effective brand of comfort which, had she known it, was winning her more friends.

Life went on. She became very much a part of the music society—an enriching experience for all. Soon she would be able to put a strategy in place to end her violent marriage.

She had made the most glorious, fulfilling connection with a good man. She was deeply in love with him. Even if their love affair was not fated to be permanent, Evan had changed her. He had made her see herself differently. She was valued and valuable; a better woman in every sense of the word.

Their relationship got better every day. Both of them had accepted their intimate commitment as lovers, and Laura derived an enormous sense of security out of their closeness. Lying together, limbs entwined, in the aftermath of love, she often felt herself on the brink of telling Evan of her horribly fresh past. How her husband had abused and terrified her. But the mere thought of destroying the happiness she and Evan had achieved together stopped her tongue.

She couldn't throw that away. Not yet. But she knew the day was fast coming when she could no longer evade the truth. It was crucial she tell him everything about the marriage she had allowed herself to be trapped in. It would be humiliating. No matter which way she looked at it, no matter the excuses she made for herself, she had lied to Evan.

But she wasn't the same person now as she had been then. Unquestionably she was stronger. Though the only way she could be totally sure was to confront Colin and survive his anger.

Some part of her lived in astonishment that he hadn't been able to trace her. She had communicated with her mother to let her now she was safe, and had discovered a tremendously angry and frustrated Colin had made the trip to New Zealand to find out what her mother knew. The meeting, with Colin's threatening demeanour for once out in the open, had upset her mother terribly. Craig, her mother's husband, had been forced to order Colin out of the house.

It was still better for her mother and Craig that they know

nothing of her whereabouts, lest Colin wreak his vengenance on them.

The front door chimes sounded through the little cottage she called home. She almost ran to the door, a spontaneous smile playing around her lips.

Evan stood outside, wearing a white T-shirt and jeans with a linen jacket on top to add a more formal touch. "Hi!" He reached out and stroked her cheek. "Ready?"

They were off to a little ceremony to bring closure to what was possibly Koomera Crossing's biggest mystery. The interment of little Estelle Sinclair.

"More than ready," she answered. "I'll just grab my handbag."

"Tell me, what do you think about all this stunning development?" he asked as they drove away.

"Estelle's is an extraordinary story. I think we'll have to accept the fact Sarah is psychic."

"She's certainly different. That Sinclair place is a thoroughly disturbing house. It has a definite aura. I often wondered why Sarah chose to live there when she returned to town. I know Kyall was very much against it, but she was adamant. You stayed there for a couple of days—anything that went bump in the night?"

"Could be, but I missed it." Laura shook her head.

"Estelle's ghost has been seen on and off for the past hundred years." He gave her a sceptical glance.

"Not by you?"

"I'm obviously too much the sceptic. Things have to be proved. The paranormal isn't exactly my area of expertise. In fact I'm dumbfounded by Sarah's story."

"The girl's bones have been found and DNA-tested," Laura pointed out. "The whole town of Koomera Crossing is turning out to see them interred. Hopefully it will bring closure to the town and to the Sinclair descendants.

"Sarah had told me her story. The house had been built in the late 1870s by a colonial architect named Robert Sinclair. His eldest daughter, Estelle, a pretty blonde girl of twelve, had simply vanished into thin air. A massive search had failed to discover any trace of her. The broken-hearted family had packed up and returned to Adelaide; Estelle's fate had never been known until Sarah went to live in the house and her strange experiences began.''

"I never liked the idea of Sarah wandering around there," Evan said. "But Sarah was born and bred in this town. She knew the local folklore better than most. The Sinclair homestead was always thought to be haunted.''

Laura looked out at the vividly coloured landscape. "It certainly sends off vibrations, I can't deny that. Sarah thinks she was *meant* to go there, even as she questioned her own motives for staying. On one occasion she told me she was standing on the verandah, waiting for Kyall to arrive, when her mind was flooded by images. She saw a girl drowning. She saw her long blonde hair. The waterhole and the boulders rising out of it. Most terrifying of all, she saw a man.

"She told me she felt incredibly frightened, as if she was being drawn into another reality. She could feel the nerve-jittering shock right through her body. She wanted to pull out of the images but they wouldn't let her go. Another time it was a dream so detailed that when she woke up she was able to identify the exact lagoon. When they were children she and Kyall used to ride all over the countryside exploring.''

"The whole thing is baffling," Evan had to concede. "Slightly uncomfortable to most people, I suppose, though there's little doubt certain individuals have 'powers' and others have paranormal experiences. The atmosphere surrounding the house was probably conducive to setting Sarah off.''

"She says she's a doctor, not a clairvoyant. She has no wish to be. What happened to her happened. There's no everyday explanation. Sarah convinced Kyall to have the waterhole searched. We all know the rest. Divers found the child's remains.''

"I would have thought the Sinclair descendants would have taken them back to Adelaide but obviously they've all agreed Estelle will be buried here at Koomera Crossing.''

Laura took a breath. "Sarah said she'd been raped and murdered.''

"Laura, we have no means of knowing that." He tossed her a searching look. "It was a dream, after all."

"A dream that turned up Estelle. The murderer went free, despite a thorough investigation."

"I'm sure Sarah wouldn't have wanted to come face to face with him," he said wryly.

"Except there's a twist. She saw his face, his features."

"Time is fleeting, Laura," he pointed out dryly. "Had this man lived, he'd be around one hundred and fifty."

"All right, all right. It's an amazing story, all the same."

Evan frowned suddenly. "I assume Sarah looked through all the old records?"

"I never asked."

"Having taken it this far, perhaps Sarah should look into it further. The whole thing's so damned odd."

Laura smiled. "I expect Sarah is fully occupied with her wedding. It's just over a week off."

"A great day! I'm looking forward to it."

"Everyone is." Laura laughed. "She has her beautiful young daughter to attend her."

Evan nodded. "A miracle in itself. Have you decided what you're going to wear?" He was seized by a vision of how she would look as a bride.

"I expect I'll have to wear something I've already got."

"Why's that?" He studied her profile, as he did when she lay sleeping at night.

"I was a bit late to ask the town dressmaker—who's simply marvelous—I've seen her things—to run me up something," she explained wryly.

"Let me see…I don't actually have anything in my wardrobe one could properly call wedding finery. Why don't we take a quick trip to Brisbane?" he suggested. "I could organise a charter flight to the nearest domestic airport. We'd have to stay a night, of course. Maybe two. What do you say?"

He glanced at her, thinking she'd be thrilled. Instead her lovely white skin had gone even whiter.

"What's the matter?" He knew his tone was taut but he

couldn't help it. He thought he had managed to seal off all the anxieties that swirled around her.

"Evan, it would cost too much money." She tried to put him off. She dared not show herself anywhere near the State capital.

"I think I can afford it. What's upsetting you? Ah, let me guess. The dreaded doctor is in Brisbane?" He fought against his disappointment and anger. "Hell, it's taken me months to find that out."

"I never said he was." Sick panic ran down her spine.

"I'm afraid you say nothing about your background. You do realise even if your doctor is having difficulty tracing you I'd have no difficulty tracing him?"

"You wouldn't!" Her heart leapt to her throat.

"Why so shocked. I thought you realised ours is no casual affair. Not for me."

"Evan, it's not casual for me either." Her eyes clouded.

"No, but there are some issues to be worked out. Clearly your doctor friend is at the top of the list. Is he married? Are you his mistress? Has he put off divorcing his wife? Are you angry about it?"

She could hear the impatience and frustration in his voice. "Evan, I love being with you."

"At the same time you're contemplating returning to this man. Oh, don't look out of the window. That's about the size of it."

"I don't feel the same about him any longer," she protested. "I want to be rid of him."

He took his eyes off the road long enough to stare at her in consternation. "Heavens, Laura, you're talking like you're already married to the guy. I don't feel like battling a shadow. I think the two of us should confront this man. Obviously he's been able to dominate you."

She bit her lip hard. Trying to rid herself of her fear of Colin was an excruciatingly difficult process. At his worst she was quite sure Colin could threaten her life. Perhaps threaten Evan's? She could be putting Evan in danger at this very moment.

"The painful fact is he did dominate my life, Evan, but that's all over. You can be absolutely sure I'll never go back to him. I don't want you to meet him either, but I think you will." Her voice was full of trepidation.

"Good," he said shortly. "Your doctor holds no fears for me. I'll make it my business to see he presents no threats to you. For your sake, I'm being as patient as I know how."

"I'm so grateful for it."

He loved her too much to continue a conversation that clearly upset her, no matter his frustration. "What about Sydney?" He returned to a much more pleasant subject. "Melbourne, if you prefer?"

"Are you doing this for you or me?"

"For both of us," he said, giving her a reassuring smile. "It just occurred to me I'd like to help you pick out your dress."

"What a wonderful idea—considering it's you I want to look beautiful for." Her face lit to radiance.

"Then it's a date." He'd come too far. Everything depended on keeping Laura safe.

During the ceremony for Estelle Sinclair many a townswoman dabbed away tears, while the descendants of the Sinclair family standing staunchly together were visibly affected. This discovery of their young ancestor was more than any of them had ever dreamt of.

They had talked to Sarah about her experiences in the house built by Estelle's father. She had told them everything she could, meeting not with scepticism but with an almost religious acceptance that Estelle's spirit had reached out to her.

This had been a terrible tragedy in the history of the Sinclair family. They all agreed they had gained much comfort from the fact she'd finally been laid to rest.

Evan and Laura stayed in one of Sydney's finest hotels, with balconies looking out over the glorious blue expanse of the Harbour. Evan had booked them discreetly into separate but adjoining rooms. Laura would talk about paying her share later. She didn't have a glimmering of knowledge about Evan's wealth, but gradually she had begun to see he had no worries whatever with money.

They had limited time, but they had already managed to tour the city and the famous Harbour. Not that Laura hadn't seen it all before, but the time she spent with Evan put her experiences on a different plane. Everything made such an impression on her it was almost as if she were reborn.

They had dinner that first night at the restaurant of her choice. It wouldn't have been the first choice of most young women bent on enjoying all the city had to offer. It was exclusive, and the food was always superb, but in the main it was an elegant haunt for the kind of people who liked and expected privacy. If one wished to be seen, or preferred more razzle-dazzle, one went elsewhere. Laura's fervent wish was to be anonymous—for very obvious reasons.

It was not to be.

They were sitting back sipping coffee when a tall, thin, very distinguished-looking man, with sharp blue eyes and a thick shock of platinum hair, paused at Evan's shoulder. He leaned over and pressed it.

"My dear Evan! How absolutely marvellous to see you. People told me you'd gone into hiding."

Ever alert for trouble, Laura looked quickly at Evan, surprising a curious expression on his face. Nevertheless he stood up, radiating his own authority. "Wonderful to see you, Sir David." He flashed his illuminating smile, reaching for the older man's extended hand. "You haven't changed a bit."

"Well, you have, my boy. You've turned into your father. Quite extraordinary! I always thought you favoured Marina's side of the family. And this beautiful young woman?"

He looked down with interest at the seated Laura, clearly charmed by her appearance. She had gone to a lot of trouble that evening to appear more sophisticated. She was wearing a silver sequinned top with a black brocade skirt, silver earrings, silver bracelet. She looked very beautiful, very expensive. She had managed to achieve the sophisticated look she was after.

"Forgive me," Evan said smoothly. "Laura, meet Sir David Ashe, one of our most distinguished diplomats. Sir David, this is a close friend of mine, Laura Graham."

"Delighted to meet you, my dear." The bright blue eyes sparkled with curiosity as Sir David bowed over Laura's hand. "Evan, I'm in Sydney for a few days," he said as he straightened. "I wonder if we could meet for an hour or so for some serious conversation? If that doesn't interfere with your plans? We simply have to catch up.

"All right, all right…" He waved an acknowledging hand at a group clearly waiting for him in the foyer. "I must go. Friends. I'm supposed to be meeting someone Very Important. What about tomorrow some time at the club?" Sir David glanced back at Laura for her okay, which she gave by gently smiling.

"I don't see why that can't be arranged, Sir David." Evan took hold of the older man's elbow. "I'll walk along with you, if I may. Back in a moment, Laura."

"Pleasure to have met you, Laura," Sir David called as he was spirited away.

So what was that all about? Laura was left to ponder. There had been nothing remotely nervous about Evan's manner. He obviously knew Sir David Ashe well, as Sir David knew him and his family, but she couldn't help realizing Evan hadn't wanted the conversation to continue.

Marina? Evan's mother's name? Marina wasn't all that usual as a Christian name. Laura's brain began to tick over. A few quite famous Marinas came to mind. And then there was Marina Kellerman, the concert cellist. She remembered seeing her perform the Elgar once, but that had been years ago, when she was a student. As far as she knew Marina Kellerman had retired, or she was teaching. She could easily find out.

But then why should she? It would be like spying on Evan. One thing she did know—his real name wasn't Thompson. Probably, had Sir David continued talking, she could have found out quite a lot. She recalled Sir David's opening remarks about people telling him Evan had gone into hiding. One would think it would be easy to open up to someone one was in love with, yet they both clung to their secrets. The past was so powerful.

Afterwards they took a taxi to the Opera House, strolling along the waterfront of Bennalong Point, the peninsula jutting out into the Harbour. Many people were about: tourists, families, young couples enjoying the balmy night and the salt breeze off the water.

The Sydney Opera House was one of the great buildings of the world, designed by the Danish architect Joern Utzon. It was all lit up, its two ''sails'' made of overlapping shells glittering under the lights.

There was a symphony concert on that evening in one of the halls, Laura knew. A ballet by a major ballet company in another. Opera in a third. Evan had asked her if she'd like to go along to any one of them but she'd declined, not wanting to risk exposure. Many of Colin's circle thought nothing of jetting down to Sydney for a special performance.

She was quiet on the way back to the hotel, giving way to introspection. Evan too seemed slightly withdrawn, which seemed ominous to her, though he was as solicitous as ever helping her out of the taxi.

At her door she hesitated, painfully aware of his body, separate from hers.

''I'll say goodnight, Evan. That was a lovely evening.''

''Don't go away.'' His eyes were jet-black with desire. ''Where's your key?''

''I'm fine.'' She half turned from him to look in her evening purse.

''No, you're not. Give it to me, Laura.'' As he said it he put his arm around her waist and pulled her in tight.

''Don't go away,'' he said again as he looked down at her. They were inside the room and she backed against the door.

How could she feel so low when only an hour ago she had been so high she soared?

Guilt was with her now, and the feelings of being trapped in a mesh of lies and half-truths. A prison of her own making.

"What is it? Tell me?" Hunger obliterated everything. He began to kiss her, one hand pressing her head to him, the other encircling her body, his mouth moving, seeking, drinking, all over her face.

She nearly fainted with the ecstasy, clinging to him now.

His mouth kept moving. Down along her throat. His strong arm half lifted her from the ground to bring her somewhere near his own height. She could hear the soft groan at the back of his throat at the pleasure she was giving him. His hand touched her breasts, shaping them through the thin sequin-encrusted chiffon. Fire shot through her. It was a miracle the chiffon didn't go up in flames.

"You can't possibly go away from me," he muttered. Then in one surge of emotion he picked her up and carried her to the bed.

"Do you love me, Evan?" she asked, her heart in her eyes.

"You've changed my whole world." He bent over her, kissed her parted mouth. "Let me show you."

Very gently, slowly, he removed her evening shoes with the little diamanté buckles, then her skirt and her cobweb-thin black tights. She stayed quiet as he did it, her heart racing so fast her short gasps ruffled the gossamer fabric of her bodice.

"What are you doing here with me?" he asked. His voice was sensuous, his eyelids heavy with the weight of desire.

"Falling in love." She said, staring back at him.

"You want to be with me, don't you?" His arm supported her as he drew off her silver top as gently as one might undress a baby.

"I adore you. How long does it take to fall in love, do you think?" She lay back on the bed, her body perfect in a filmy black lace bra and briefs.

"Less than a minute?" He turned to strip off his jacket, throw away his royal blue silk tie, while she watched him in fascination. His chest was so broad. Powerful.

He came back to the bed, leaned over her. The pressure to

make love to her was building, expanding like great wings in his chest. Her fragrance rose into his nostrils. He could breathe it in on his pillow. She was all the woman he could ever want, yet despite all his nurturing she was keeping things from him—as indeed he was keeping things from her. It had to change if their relationship was to go where he fervently wanted it to go.

"Love is what's happened to me. Love at first sight." He lay down beside her, instinct telling him it was important to her that he guide her into the tempestuous open sea of ecstasy. He pulled her close, whispered endearments into her ear.

His voice possessed the flavour of rich black coffee. She felt his hand move over her cleavage, linger as he gently undid her bra, continuing to caress her all the time.

No panic. Never any panic with Evan. Never any feelings of desperation that she couldn't make things work. Evan didn't lunge at her without warning. He was never violent. Though the response he aroused in her was so deeply passionate he might have been a highly skilled magician. He told her how lovely she was, how pretty were her hands and her feet as he kissed them. Colin had never done anything like that.

Now Evan's hands were moving over the whole naked length of her, gently separating her legs. The room was blurring around her, though she could see his face, expression intense, the muscles along his strong jawline taut with sexual urgency. Her body was crying out for him. She strained closer. She wanted him deep inside her. She wanted to reach the sweet, fierce, soaring climax she had never reached with Colin. She wanted release.

His hands were beneath her, lifting her up onto his body, his mouth reaching for her pink nipple as he drew her down onto him, then up, her insides contracting with pleasure.

A great tide of emotion came for her, gathering force. Spontaneously she arched her body as they established a rhythm, her head thrown back in rapture, hair flying around them like silk, all the warm juices in her body flowing like nectar. She had a sense of losing herself entirely, and then she heard Evan calling her name.

Laura!

So beautiful on his tongue.

The ripples started in stealth, building until they began to rush over her in a huge tumbling liquid plume.

"Do you want me?" he found himself muttering harshly maddened beyond endurance. He had never in his life felt like this. She was everything his body and mind sought.

"I want everything about you," Laura cried out, before sensation upon sensation overwhelmed her, reducing her to soft whimpers.

When Laura reopened her eyes it was to a darkened room.

"Evan?" She threw out an arm to affirm he was there.

"I'm here." He came in from the balcony, where he'd been standing, thinking, while looking out at the night.

"What time is it?" She sat up.

"Three. I never fail to wake around three."

"Have you something on your mind? Please come back to me." He was the answer to her prayers. Still naked, she began to search for her robe. Evan was wearing the white towelling robe supplied by the hotel.

"No, leave it. I love you naked," he said in his low thrilling voice.

"Is something worrying you?" She lifted her arms, wanting only to offer him comfort.

"Not really, Laura." He slipped into the bed beside her, one arm gathering her against him, her head tucked into the bow of his shoulder, the satiny warmth of her breasts against his heart. "But I think the time has come to be honest. You didn't like what happened tonight with Sir David suddenly appearing out of the blue?"

"Only that he knows all about you, which I clearly don't. He knows your family, your mother, Marina. How you resemble the father you lost. He knows your name. Is it Kellerman?" She knew it was before he answered.

He stroked her silky head. "You're very good."

"I can put a puzzle together if I get a few clues. Your mother is Marina Kellerman, the concert cellist?"

"Yes," he admitted with pride. "My mother taught me to play. I told you that. My father was Christian Kellerman. He was a career diplomat. A very good one, like Sir David, but he was posted to dangerous places. He was killed in the Balkans some years back. It was a terrorist attack. The woman I thought I was in love with—"

"Monika?" She felt a short painful stab of jealousy.

"Monika, yes." His tone hardened. "Monika betrayed his precise itinerary to a terrorist gang she was working under-cover for. She had infiltrated the freedom fighters who trusted me and were keeping me informed. I am—or was—as you suspected a foreign correspondent. The great tragedy is, even with my experience, I trusted Monika—as did a lot of other people. It cost my father and his driver, a man called Thompson, their lives. I've never forgiven myself, though my mother told me constantly I was not to blame."

Laura lifted her head to gaze at him. "Evan, how very terrible! Your pain shows."

"You can attribute that to the horror I've seen. In those days I was a risk-taker. Anything to get a good story. But I had the fear of God drummed into me. I lived through terrible times. Times it might take me for ever to talk about. After I got home, I guess you could say I had a breakdown. My mother held me together through the worst times. We're very close. But there was so much conflict inside me. So much guilt, I had to get away. Far away. I worshipped my father. Finally I hit on here, to be near the desert. I thought I needed the desert to heal."

"You couldn't tell anyone outside your mother? A coun-sellor? Some very insightful person?" Her own abuse seemed unremarkable in the light of this.

"I couldn't begin to speak of my experiences, much like a war veteran can't. War is terrible. The loss, the fear, the large-scale slaughter, the inhumanity. I saw so much cruelty and death I just wanted to block it out. But I couldn't block out thoughts of my father. And poor old Thompson, the innocent victim. Thompson was devoted to Dad. They ended their lives together.''

"So you took his name. I'm so sorry, Evan." She touched his face, his throat with a slow flowing hand full of sympathy and understanding.

"I hated Monika." He caught her hand and carried it passionately to his mouth. "I think I'd have killed her—only someone else did the job."

She swallowed hard. "If you had you wouldn't have been here for me." Laura hesitated. "How often do you think of her?"

"I wasn't in love with her, Laura. I didn't even know her. The real Monika I hated. She used her beauty as a weapon. I didn't know what love between a man and a woman was. Monika had courage, but she was evil. While I would have gone to the ends of the earth for a good story she would have done anything to gain power and influence for herself. Needless to say power went along with money."

"And I reminded you of her?" Laura was dismayed.

"Momentarily. Until I looked into your beautiful eyes. Monika is part of the past. Gone for ever. I would trust you with my life."

Her heart clamped. Would he feel like that in the light of her own disclosures? "Do you think you have begun to heal?"

"I know so." He dropped a hungry kiss on her mouth. "You've brought back the beauty to my life. I really needed help but I didn't know where to start looking. How was I to even dream help would come from the girl next door?" he asked with tender humour.

"Then I've achieved something worthwhile in my life." Even if things went badly in the future, if psychotic Colin should be the end of her, she would be left with the magical time she and Evan had spent together.

"You could say that, love of mine. I feel incredibly blessed to have met you."

"Please don't put me on a pedestal, Evan," she warned.

"As though you could betray me." He stared down at her,

wanting her desperately again. "I need you and you need me. You're not cold?" he asked, as she shivered slightly.

"A tiny bit."

"I'll soon cure that. I'm burning away myself. Only for you." He took her cool, slender body fully into his arms. "Do you think you could bear more lovemaking?"

She let her arm encircle his beloved head as her lips formed the exquisite word. "Yes!"

Those starved of love can't get enough.

CHAPTER TWELVE

KOOMERA Crossing was *en fête*. Today was the wedding day of two of the town's favourite people. Kyall McQueen, master of the historic station Wunnamurra, and Sarah Dempsey, head of Koomera Crossing Bush Hospital. Both had been born and bred in their beloved Channel Country, and now they were to be finally united as man and wife.

The guest list numbered over three hundred. Those who hadn't made it weren't left out. A day-into-evening party had been organised for the townspeople in the main street. All traffic had been blocked off. Brightly coloured bunting flew from the shopfronts and crisscrossed the street. Long trestle tables and chairs had been set up. Piped music had been organized.

Celebrations would start with a magnificent brunch, the beef, the veal, the lamb and the pork supplied by Wunnamurra Station. There were to be savoury dishes galore, with all the accompaniments. Mexican-style chilli, favourite pizzas, pies and pastas, salads. Jumbo desserts.

All in praise of the legendary McQueen family, whose financial generosity for well over a century had made the town what it was.

Mrs Ruth McQueen, now dead, had fought for the town hospital—in the process saving many lives. Everyone acknowledged this freely. But no one wanted her back. So far as the town was concerned her grandson Kyall was the right candidate for taking over the many business concerns. Overnight he had become heir to the family fortune, with all the right talents to make his grand inheritance and the town grow. He deserved his beautiful bride.

It came into Laura's mind that this day, so blissful for Sarah and Kyall and their lovely daughter Fiona, so recently discovered, would have a different outcome for her.

Nonetheless she dressed with excitement in the outfit she and
Evan had settled on from a choice of three—Evan at the
outset had said with such enthusiasm, "That's exactly you!"
and had made her and the saleswoman laugh.

The dress, a lovely jacaranda into violet chiffon, was
printed with deep pink full-blown roses and buds with sprays
of silver-green leaves, its style paying homage to the graceful
cocktail gowns of the 1920s. The sleeveless bodice dipped
low. The ankle-length hem of the skirt was trimmed with fine
silvery-green lace. There were violet silk and lace sandals to
match; an exquisite pink silk rose for her hair. It was a very
lyrical look, very feminine. A style that suited her better than
any other.

In the old ballroom of the homestead, that had been turned
into a flower-decked chapel, Sarah and Kyall made their
vows before the visiting Bishop.

As the Bishop began the traditional words of the wedding
ceremony, and the congregation of wedding guests dissolved
into a reverent silence, Laura felt the tears rising to her eyes.
She couldn't fail to remember her own wedding day. Her
ravishing white satin gown, miles of skirt, her cathedral-
length veil held in place by an antique diamond and pearl
diadem lent to her by her mother-in-law—to be returned the
same day—her bouquet of white rosebuds… She had gone
to her husband a virgin. He had done such things to her. Was
it any wonder she felt shame? The man she now knew she
loved, Evan, stood beside her, his height and powerful build
making him look regal in his wedding finery, his dark head
slightly bowed as if to say these were serious and solemn
moments.

God protect them, Laura thought as she rejoiced in the
bride and groom's happiness. They were already a family.
Complete. To one side stood their young daughter in her
wedding finery, a cream silk-tulle dress with crystal embroi-
dery on the full floating skirt. Sarah, the bride, wore the palest
shade of gold, a simple garland of yellow and cream roses
in her magnificent golden hair. She looked heavenly.

Did I look heavenly? Laura thought, falling into a sad little

reverie. People said I did. Even Colin's parents had beamed
on her as a suitable bride for their son.

What did they think of her now? She could imagine the
lies Colin had fed them. No one could be more persuasive.
Not that his parents would need much convincing. It would
be far too painful, too grievous, for them to consider their
only son was less than perfect, much less a wife-beater.

The ceremony over, the walls of guests milled all over the
house—the ballroom and reception rooms, the huge entrance
hall that formed the heart of the house—spilling out onto the
broad verandahs and down into the homestead's grounds, a
parkland manicured for the great occasion.

Two giant white marquees had been set up for the sumptuous reception at which Kyall spoke so lovingly and mov-
ingly of his love for his bride, the magic of their wedding
day, the miracle of being reunited with their child. Laura and
Harriet, who sat at the same table, had difficulty holding back
the tears.

"This is what I've always wanted," Harriet, resplendent
in gold with big pearls around her neck, whispered to Laura.
"For Sarah and Kyall to be happily married."

Mitchell Claydon, so very dashing, with an intriguing dim-
ple in one cheek, made everyone laugh. Then Kyall's beautiful sister, Christine, spoke in warm, honeyed tones that had
more than a suggestion of an American accent about the
childhood of all four, Sarah and Kyall, she and Mitch, and
the applause overflowed.

It was a time for high emotion for all. Sarah came to them
and they all hugged her, hugged Sarah's daughter, Fiona, so
much the image of her mother it took the breath away.

"Isn't this the most marvellous day?" Fiona cried exu-
berantly, her arm around her mother's waist, clinging to her.
"And I'm going on the honeymoon!"

"We couldn't bear to leave her." Sarah smiled radiantly
at everyone, embracing her daughter. Then Sarah in turn was
surrounded by other groups of people who wanted to wish
her all the happiness in the world.

The sun was a great golden ball, the sky a cloudless imperial royal blue. As Laura and Evan strolled down to the green crystal creek that wound its way lazily through the home gardens Evan laid a gentle hand on Laura's arm, slowing her progress.

"What is it, sweetheart? Are those tears of joy, or what?" He couldn't help but be aware she was very emotional.

"It's been an amazing experience," she sighed. "There's so much love between them."

"There is, and it's wonderful, but why so sad?"

"You know me too well." She turned to walk a few feet.

"Sometimes, my love, I think I don't know you at all," he said wryly.

"But you like what you do know?" She stopped beneath a shade tree covered with purple buds.

"I *love* what I do know." His tone held astonishing warmth. "I've waited quite a while for you to confide in me. I guess I can hang on a bit longer."

"You must!" Her voice broke a little with emotion. Colin couldn't be allowed to threaten them. "Evan, I love you so much." He was her strength, her security.

"So why are we wasting time?" He turned her to face him. Flames flared in his dark eyes. "I want a future together. I want a loving, stable relationship. I want marriage. Children. Do you want children, Laura?"

She caught a blossom as it fell, inhaling its sweet perfume. "I love children. The sweetest thing in the world is a baby."

"You never mention your doctor any more."

"So don't remind me."

"Not on this festive day, but clearly he's an issue that has to be settled."

"I know that, Evan."

"Your feelings for him drove you out here. I saw how unhappy you were. I can feel the sadness in you today."

"Then I'm going to make up my mind to be happy," she promised him. "I am happy." She lifted her glossy, rose-adorned head to meet his ardent gaze. "You're so very, very, important to me. I long more than anything in the world for us to be together."

"Then we will."

"No matter what?" She felt her heart crack.

"No matter what."

"Promise?" she begged, putting a hand to the lapel of his pearl-grey jacket, fancying she could hear the beat of his heart.

He was mad to kiss her.

In full view of the strolling guests he bent his head, muttering, "I do," into her sweet open mouth.

"Then that's that!"

Evan wanted just two things. To love her. To look after her. Whatever involvement she had with her ex-lover, he was going to bring it to an end.

He knew he only had to pick up the phone to track the man down. After all the news stories he'd broken, finding Laura's mystery doctor would be a piece of cake. No difficulty either finding out Laura's true identity. Her background.

Only love for her and the feeling he would be intruding on her right to privacy held him in check. He had been talking about their trip to the Red Centre a week later. She would have her chance to confide in him then.

To Laura's mind the beauty of the mighty monolith Uluru was most fully appreciated at sunset, when the sun moving down over the horizon created the most spectacular colour effects on the western wall.

She watched entranced as the immense rock with its wonderfully sculptured contours went through its phenomenal colour display. This was truly one of the great wonders of the natural world, she thought with fascination, unchanged in form for an awesome forty million years. Uluru dominated the great desert of Spinifex and sand that stretched as far as the eye could see.

They had watched the Rock at sunrise too, when the vast shadowy outline slowly became illuminated. Its sheer size, its strength and aura of great antiquity, held the watcher spellbound. When the sun first appeared on the horizon the crest began to glow a gentle pink that turned to rose. As the sun rose further into the sky the entire dome turned golden-red, at which point Laura had not only felt like cheering but she had, to Evan's pleasure and amusement.

The wonderful bird-life that so characterized the Outback and offered its own fascination had suddenly taken wing, as if to salute it, and by noon the Rock had begun to blend with the fiery sand.

Driving back to their motel, some twenty-five kilometres away, it had appeared in the distance, Namitjira's larkspur.

But now, at sunset! The island-mountain went through its most magnificent displays, the colours deeper, richer—the glowing golden orange of a fire's embers, blazing terracotta-red, and then, as the sun began to sink, the Rock turned a soft velvety mauve, purple in the folds, the deep shadows at its base creating the illusion that the mighty monolith was floating above ground.

Evan, one arm around her shoulder, remarked quietly, "Easy to understand how the Rock is such a sacred cere- monial place for the aboriginals. The caves around the base are considered to be shrines."

They had been privileged to examine the hundreds of rock paintings decorating the walls. The numerous Dreamtime leg- ends associated with the Rock, most known only to the tribal people, commemorated the exploits of their totemic ances- tors.

Laura, mindful that the tribal elders, the guardians of Uluru, didn't appreciate tourists climbing all over their holy place, had elected to view the mighty monolith from the ground.

"My father and I climbed it when I was sixteen," Evan told her. "I'll probably never get to see the summit again, but the panorama from the top was worth all the effort. You can see sheer across the desert to the Musgrave, Mann and Petermann ranges to the south, the Gil ranges and the salt lake Amadeus to the north. All those minarets, cupolas and domes we can see in the distance, some thirty kilometres west, are the Olgas. The Pitjantjatjara named them Kata Tjuta—many heads. We'll visit them tomorrow.

"Some people think they're even more spectacular than Uluru. They turn on the same colour displays, but at certain times when the winds are howling through the ravines Kata Tjuta can be a very forbidding place. Tourists are forbidden to visit Kata Tjuta after dark anyway. It was the explorer Giles who said the Olgas were more wonderful and grotesque, the Rock more ancient and sublime. I think he got it right. The aboriginal people agree.

"Far off to the east is the majestic crown of Mount Connor, another island-mountain. The Rock is a formidable climb. In some places the angle of ascent is something like sixty degrees, and with the wind blowing!"

"Why do men like to climb everything?" she asked, giving him an impulsive hug because he was so very dear to her. "Why do they go off to the Poles, risking death, stand on the rim of active volcanos, peering down into the abyss. Women would find it absolutely terrifying, even insane."

He smiled to himself. "No one has come up with a better answer than Mallory's comment when asked why he wanted to climb Mount Everest. 'Because it's there.'"

"But Everest killed Mallory. I thought it terrible, the publication of photographs of his body when it was found seventy-five years later. It seemed like a violation. I was shocked."

He shrugged. "Obviously the media was going for maximum impact, maximum drama, but that went over the line. Tired?" he asked solicitously.

"Not in the least." She shook her head. "I'm having the most wonderful time, but I am hungry."

"That's good." He took in her lovely colour, wanting nothing but to make her happy. "The air's like wine. And a bit of exertion always makes one hungrier. The food's good at the restaurant.

"We'll come back one day and see the Rock under rain," he promised her as they were driving away. "As you can imagine it doesn't happen all that often, but it's an unforgettable sight. The Rock turns a glittering metallic grey, and all the gullies on top fill with water, turning into rock pools.

Cascades of water rush down the ravines, forming beautiful white waterfalls. The green belt you see around the base of the Rock is the result of the big run-offs during the rains.''

''This is a magic place,'' Laura said.

''It is.''

''I'm going to hold you to your promise,'' Laura warned him, so happy for a moment she all but forgot the spectre of Colin.

''No need.'' He smiled at her. ''When I say we're going to do something, we will.''

As supremely spiritual as Laura had found Uluru, she was astonished by the Olgas—Kata Tjuta. A true romantic, she was captivated by the thirty or more magnificent dome-shaped monoliths separated by deep ravines, clustering over some thirty-five kilometres of desert floor.

They were a fantastic sight silhouetted against the cloud-less blue sky, glowing a jewel-bright red at the time they arrived. She had never expected the domes to be so high. Quite a few rose much higher than Uluru, which she knew was over a thousand feet. On that particular day they were blessed by the weather conditions. The frightening winds that so affected the atmosphere were in abeyance. Only a gentle breeze blew through the ravines.

''Well, what do you think?'' Evan asked, smiling quietly at the fascinated expression on her face. This beautiful young woman, his lover. It must have been destined she would conquer his heart.

''The domes are so extraordinary they've stolen my breath away. How would you describe them?''

''Again I don't think you could beat Giles's 'rounded min-arets, giant cupolas and monstrous domes'. They're like the ruins of some fabulous ancient city, built by giants for giants.''

''I'm surprised by their height. In the distance they didn't appear so very tall.''

He came behind her, resting his hands on her shoulders,

caressing the fine bones. "Perfectly flat desert plain," he explained. "No trees or hills to give perspective."

"And it's greener." Laura lifted her head as a great flight of budgerigar in a long V formation flashed emerald-green and gold over her head.

"The deep ravines provide enough shade to retain rainwater over long periods, consequently Kata Tjuta supports a large animal population. Most of them live among the domes without even venturing out onto the desert plains."

"Wonderful things have happened to me." She sighed blissfully, resting back against him.

"More wonderful things are in store," he promised, letting his hands drop to the tender swell of her breasts.

At about the same time Laura and Evan were making love in the wild splendour of the desert Dr Colin Morcombe was poring over a magazine his receptionist had brought to his attention. Insufferable bitch, he would sack her, he thought, detesting the humiliation.

It was Laura, of course. Lovely little Laura, looking as pretty as a picture at Sarah Dempsey's wedding. She looked radiantly happy, which was more of a shock.

I don't believe it! A terrible rage broke over him, otherwise he would have laughed and laughed. He'd been convinced her mother was hiding her somewhere in New Zealand, where he had a private investigator still on the job, costing an arm and a leg. And who was the big, tall dark-haired bastard standing so possessively behind her? Every instinct told him the two of them were having a relationship. It was all in the body language. He knew about such things.

Unfaithful bitch! he raged, wanting to kill them. Not enough to leave me; you betray me as well.

It had been a huge shock to him when Laura had found the guts to run away. He had convinced himself she was too soft, too weak. The ideal victim. How he missed her! Her soft flesh. He had never got over his insatiable hunger for her. Women were goddesses—or devils.

What he was seeing now was Laura the betrayer. He could

kill her. Take that white throat between his hands and squeeze and squeeze. Only he'd have her first.

The thought brought up little quivers all over his spine. He was one step away from arousal. Only lovely Laura with her soft pleading voice could do that to him. Only with Laura did he have power. With other women, more brash and worldly, at the last minute he'd be stricken impotent. The humiliation was terrible, though they pretended to laugh it off. He needed to have power. Control. He needed to intimidate. That was what it was all about.

Power!

The wall clock in his room infuriated him with its endless ticking. He sat at his desk, his hands, his very clever hands, pressed over his ears. His nurse came to the door, peered in, obviously about to say something—but he glared at her. At least she had the sense to murmur an apology and shut the door. She wasn't like that bloody receptionist. She wouldn't run out and tell everyone something was definitely wrong with the doctor.

Only it was!

Laura deserved to be punished. She deserved to be taught a lesson. One she would never forget.

He was a very busy man, with a big operation scheduled for three days' time. None of that mattered. He'd get Romsey to do it. He was so enraged that for a moment he didn't realize he was thrusting his letter-opener into his palm. He flung it away, narrowly missing a cut-glass paperweight.

''God, the bitch!'' he whispered, though his anger was like a roar in his head. Tears of self-pity began to pour down his face. He'd teach her a lesson she'd remember all her life. ''You're going to be sorry, Laura.''

As for her lover? He drove a fist into his chest. From the size of him, the look of him, he wasn't a man to take on in broad daylight. But there was always the cover of darkness.

He reached for his handkerchief and wiped his face furiously. What he had to do was send someone out to that God-forsaken place. What was the name of the town? Koomera Crossing?

Of course he remembered Sarah Dempsey, so beautiful there in her wedding dress. It cut like hell that she'd been part of this. A fellow doctor, goddamn her! And now she had a powerful husband to protect her. There weren't too many people in the State who hadn't heard of the McQueens. They were too big to touch, otherwise meddling Sarah would get what was coming to her.

The thought suddenly crossed his mind that they might be waiting for him. Laura's abusive husband. Wouldn't little Laura tell a sob story! What he had to do was send someone to check out the town. They had to be quick. It said here McQueen was on his honeymoon. The lover must be lured away. He needed Laura isolated...

CHAPTER THIRTEEN

THE night before they left the desert Laura woke up in a cold sweat, her heart drumming in her ears.

She'd had a dream. A terrible dream. Chaotic.

She was back in Thailand, the scene of her honeymoon. Colin was pursuing her through a darkened temple, though she could see the glimmering of a river through the windows of the huge wooden building. Numbers of living Buddhas, skin gleaming gold, richly attired, jewel-adorned, were all around her, seated and walking, accompanied by monks in their saffron robes. She could see them all vividly. She threw out her hands, imploring them to hide her within the temple, but they moved slowly past her as though she were invisible or had no voice.

Colin was the hunter. She was the hunted. Incapable as always of overcoming her fear of him and his punishing hands. She ran out of the temple into a shrill and tumultuous thoroughfare, swarming with Asians and the little three-wheeled tuk-tuks that transported tourists. Nobody looked at her as she ran crying for help. Nobody spoke to her. By now she was frantic.

She ran to a great carved and decorated door. At last she would find sanctuary. She pulled on the brass handle. The door didn't budge. She rattled the handle, pulling with all her strength. Panting, struggling, she managed to get it to give a little—only Colin was behind her, overpowering her.

She threw up her hands to protect her face, screaming out helplessly, ''No! No! No!'' without any will left to fight.

''Open your eyes, Laura. Open them!'' a voice ordered her.

''No, I don't want to.'' She tried to get away.

''Laura! You're dreaming. Open your eyes. It's me, Evan. I won't let anything hurt you.''

157

"Oh…Evan!" She turned onto her back, releasing her sti-
fled breath. Dazedly she stared up into his strongly hewn
face. "Oh, God! My heart is pounding so hard I could be
sick."

"It was a nightmare," he told her, smoothing her damp
tumbled hair off her face. "Just a nightmare. You're safe
now."

"Ahh!" She had to wait for her heart to slow.

Evan turned away to snap on the light. He stared down at
her with jet-black intensity. She looked deeply disturbed, a
fine dew of sweat sheened her lovely skin. Desert nights were
very cold, but their room was air conditioned, set at a comfortable temperature. He rose and walked to the bathroom.
Quickly he found a face washer, wetting it thoroughly, then
wringing it out.

"What was that all about?" he asked, gently, wiping her
face, her throat and her hands before patting them dry. "I
thought one of the mythical Dreamtime creatures was trying
to grab you." He tried for a light touch though he felt quite
perturbed.

"I can't say just yet." She fought hard to break free of
the effects of the nightmare. "Do you think I could have a
glass of water?"

"Of course you can." He went away to get it, by which
time she had hauled herself up in the bed, her head leaning
back against the wall.

"There's a nip of brandy, if you want it."

"I'll be all right."

"I think I'll have one," he said, going to the small bar.
"You sounded so terrified you terrified *me*."

"It was so real!" she breathed.

"Here, let me put this rug around you." He picked up the
velvety soft rug that lay like a coverlet at the end of the bed.

She allowed him to wrap it around her, but when he went
to walk away she caught at his hand.

"Don't go, Evan."

"I'm not going anywhere, my love. I'll get my drink and
come back to bed."

"Please." She was wide awake now, but still nervous, still a part of her dream.

When Evan returned to bed he gathered her into his arms, settling her head on his chest. She inched even closer, making him bend his head to kiss her.

"Feel better now?" He stroked and soothed her, his deep voice full of concern.

"I think I'm going to pieces." She tried to laugh.

"Why? You've been so happy. We've had a wonderful time, haven't we?"

"I want it to go on for ever, but it can't."

"Why do you say that, Laura?" Driven by something in her tone, he turned up her face, held it to him.

"There's something I have to tell you, Evan," she said in a bravely determined voice.

"Then you'd better tell me. I'm ready to listen."

"I pray I'll say it well. I'm so frightened of losing you. You're the best thing that has ever happened to me. My world. I can't bear the idea of it collapsing."

Anxiety dug its claws into him, but he didn't allow it to overcome him. "I guess it's got a lot to do with your boyfriend. You'd better tell me."

Laura drew herself out of his arms. She feared outright rejection. "He's not my boyfriend, Evan. I've allowed you to believe that. Forgive me. He's my husband."

Here it comes, she thought in misery. Disbelief. Disgust. Rejection. She braced herself.

"Your husband!" Evan's voice was more full of pain than anger. "My God, Laura. Why would you keep anything so significant to our relationship to yourself?"

"I'm a coward, that's why," she said simply. "Full of fears to this day, when I've been trying desperately to get strong."

"To think I believed you!" He rose from the bed. Abandoned her. "Has this whole damn thing been a charade? I've never had an affair with a married woman before."

"I wanted to tell you, Evan."

"What else haven't you told me?" he retorted, turning to

stare at her, even now under her spell. Hell, was he stupid, besotted, or what? "A couple of kids?"

"Colin never wanted children. It was enough to have me. You had your secrets, Evan," she pointed out quietly.

"I did get around to telling you," he replied in a clipped voice. "My secrets didn't include being married." He stalked to the wardrobe, pulled out some clothes.

"What are you doing?" She stared at him almost fearfully.

"I'm going for a walk." His tone held a deep, quiet anger.

"Now?" He left her reeling with guilt.

"Yes, now," he said crisply. "Lock the door after me. You'll be perfectly safe."

"You can't bear to be with me another minute, can you?" She rose swiftly, letting the enveloping rug fall to the floor, her slender body barely veiled by her satin nightgown.

"I need a break, Laura." He looked away from her, angry that he had allowed himself to fall so deeply in love with her. "The fact you're married—and no matter what you say you can't bring yourself to break free of that marriage— changes everything for me. I hope to God you're not playing games." Memories of Monika and her betrayal suddenly battered him.

"Never." She shook her head, while her hair foamed like silk around her pale face. "Everything I've said to you came from the heart."

"Don't start crying," he warned.

"I won't." Her voice broke.

"I just have to get some air." He picked up a wool-lined jacket and put it on.

"I'm so sorry, Evan."

"I dare say you are," he said in an ironic voice. "I'd like to say let's put it behind us and move on. Except I can't."

"You have every right to be angry."

"Laura, stop.'

But she rushed to him, laying a white hand on his sleeve. "I have to tell you something else that might make you understand."

"You *do* have a child, for all your denials?" He stared down at her, his voice taking on a bitter edge. "Why should I be surprised? Does your child look like you or its father?" he asked with black humour.

"Please—there's no child. I could never leave my child." She put up her arms to him, her green eyes imploring.

"Don't!" He dragged her arms down. "It's all falling apart."

"I won't let it! I need you desperately."

In the midst of his disillusionment desire was devouring him from within. Love was like the open sea. Sometimes tranquil, other times hit by violent storms. He lifted her almost brutally high into his arms, plundering her soft cushiony mouth in a way she wasn't likely to forget. Wild thoughts, initiated by anger and passion, flashed into his head. He tightened his hold on her beautiful body, then he remembered how small she was. He might bruise her.

"Goddamn it to hell!" he muttered fiercely, letting her slide to the floor. In a heartbeat his anger faded to self-disgust. "Go back to bed, Laura. I'm sorry if I hurt you. But don't even attempt to try to seduce me again."

He started to the door, a big, angry disillusioned man, leaving Laura, trembling and bereft, staring after him. The door closed with a very loud click.

Exit Evan from my life, Laura thought fatalistically, dropping to her knees like a penitent.

But he doesn't know the half of it, a quiet, authoritative voice in her head told her, promising hope. You made a bad job of telling him. He's shocked, hurt, feeling betrayed. You can understand that, can't you? You've steeled yourself for it. Evan's a man who feels things deeply. He's taken this hard, the loss of trust. You know he wants you. As lovers you've experienced overwhelming rapture.

Pray God it was enough. She had to reach out to him again. She had to keep a straight head. Get focused on what she wanted to say. She'd been the victim of marital abuse. He must know what that meant. She'd lived in fear of her husband, who'd sworn he would follow her to the ends of the earth should she ever try to escape. Shocking when one thought about it. One human being terrorizing another.

Her flight from reality was over. In a curious way she knew relief. She had come a long way with Evan. Her new-found courage was a wavering thing. But even if she had to put herself in real physical danger she was going to confront Colin.

Hold onto that, Laura, the voice in her head urged her.

It was only much later that Laura came to believe the voice she heard that night was the voice of her beloved father.

When he returned he found she had fallen into an exhausted sleep. The thin strap of her nightgown had fallen off her shoulder, exposing the beauty and delicacy of her breasts. She was lying in a near abandoned position, one arm flung above her head, the other wide, the hem of her long night-gown rucked up on one side to reveal a straight slender leg. What lovely limbs she had! Petite of stature but everything in proportion.

He'd had this crazy dream they could make a go of it. He felt a mixture of grief and a hard self-contempt. It was sheer coincidence Laura had a look of Monika. What he had felt for Monika was nothing compared to this feeling he had for Laura. It consumed him. But he couldn't handle the fact she was married. Deception versus reality.

Yet there was so much excitement in looking at her. He backed away from the bed to a chair, slumping into it. The sun was rising over the desert, turning the eternal sands and all the great monuments pink into rose, into orange-gold.

They would have breakfast and be on their way. After that? He closed his eyes for a few moments, falling deeper into a brooding melancholy with no wish to control it.

Why wouldn't the husband, poor devil, come after her? Wouldn't he himself? The husband was probably just as madly in love with her as he was. Any man looking at her would describe her as wonderfully alluring. It was a combination of innocence and a powerful but elegant sex appeal.

He'd thought he was so damned experienced in the ways

of the world. Well, he'd been tricked by his own perceptions. He'd been so sure she was exactly what he thought she was. So sure of what went on between them. The passion and the tenderness, the euphoria that came with believing one had found one's soul mate.

He'd all but finished his book. It was good. Real. Her influence had been far-reaching. He'd wanted to return to life. Not life as he had lived it, on the extreme edge, but a new life, with Laura. She'd become his world. A world more vivid than he, world-traveller, had ever known.

Now this!

Secrets, secrets, secrets! Yet who had taught her to fear?

Only then did he start to consider the source of her obvious problems. Unless she was the world's greatest actress—and she might be—he was convinced she hadn't been treated properly. He held the image of her as she'd come out of her dream. She'd been terrified. On the brink of blind panic.

Of what? He hadn't really let her speak. There had been so much bitterness and disillusionment on his own palate.

Didn't hope spring eternal? No sooner had he come to the decision he must follow his own direction than he was back to trying to make a meaning of all that had gone between them. He remembered her saying once she wasn't good at making love. Now, that was really ridiculous.

But was it a deeply ingrained taunt? Had her husband allowed her to believe that? Tried to fool her into thinking it was the truth? She was a dream to make love to. A man could savour the experience for ever. One reason suggested itself. The husband wanted her entirely to himself. He wanted her easily manipulated, controlled. Yet the marriage bond seemed strong. It was a real puzzle.

"Evan?"

He turned his face to her. She was sitting up in the bed, watching him, her beautiful cascade of hair almost black against the white bedlinen, her green eyes shimmering like jewels in the dawn glow.

He straightened slightly in his chair. "You're awake.

"I have been for some minutes," she admitted. "You were so deep in thought I didn't like to disturb you."

His laugh was off key. "Well, you've made a thoroughly good job of that."

"I was wrong." She was out of bed, shouldering into her ivory satin robe.

"Laura, if you're going to tell me you must go back to your husband, please let it alone," he said wearily. "I thought we were celebrating the love of a lifetime, but maybe it was just one hell of an affair."

"Don't insult both of us," she said. "I need you to know precisely what went wrong with my marriage. Why I felt little guilt loving you. Only then can you judge me."

She walked towards him, with no hint of the thrilling, unconscious seductiveness that always left him tingling. She looked like a woman hell-bent on holding nothing back.

"You won't want to hear this," she said in a low, perfectly steady voice, taking the armchair beside him. "And to tell it will only cause me pain and humiliation. But it must be said. I was an abused wife. Physically, mentally, emotionally. The ugly truth. I don't want to talk about it at all, but I must. You need to understand what drove me to break my vows.

"The vows were meaningless. Colin turned his back on them the same day we made them. The abuse began on my honeymoon and continued for almost a year. Finally I found the courage to escape and come here. I felt so battered I'd almost resigned myself to a life on the run.

"You might say I should have gone for help. Once I went to a friend, but Colin persuaded her I was the one having problems. He's super-convincing. I could have gone to lawyers. But wherever I went I knew he was going to find me. He's been concentrating his attentions on my mother in New Zealand, certain she's helping me hide. But he's not giving up. Until I confront him I'll never have any peace of mind."

It was the easiest thing in the world to change one's appearance, he thought, lightly fingering his dark moustache into position. He thought he actually looked better with dark hair.

It made for a startling contrast with his eyes. Of course he'd had to mask his natural elegance. He wore the Outback tourist's ordinary gear. Bush shirt, jeans, high boots, warm coat for the evenings.

He smiled to himself every time he put on his black akubra, which he'd punched into well-worn shape. People might have remarked on his skin colour, which was pale, so he'd invested in some fake tan. He sure as hell was handsome with smoothly polished gold skin. But he had to hide these qualities a little, letting his beard grow into a fuzz, pulling the akubra down over his head.

He'd been in town—or rather on the outskirts of town—in a caravan park for two days. His dark blue Mercedes was in the garage at home. He was driving around in a dusty four-wheel drive, the tyres caked in red mud. It looked a bit on the battered side, which was what he wanted, but it was in tip-top condition. If they had to get away he had to do it right.

He knew where they'd been. According to the information he had received Ayers Rock. How absurd. He'd never thought Laura the type to go bush. He knew they were home. He knew where they lived. God, could you believe it? Side by side.

He'd driven past—fairly fast the first time. Some old girl had been coming out of the front door, probably taking care of the place in Laura's absence. The second, he'd taken his time. So his darling pampered wife had rejected his state-of-the-art home for some pitiful worker's cottage that looked more like a doll's house? God, it had made him so angry he'd had to stop and massage his temples.

At least the private investigator he'd sent out here had done a good job. He'd found out more than where they lived. Something unexpected. The guy's name. Amazing what one could learn from a photograph. Evan Kellerman, not Evan Thompson as the town knew him. And his darling little unfaithful wife. Laura Graham. He'd only just recently discovered Laura's mother's maiden name.

He had succeeded in getting a ticket for a concert they

were giving tonight. How many top-flight foreign correspondents—and apparently Kellerman had made quite a reputation for himself—also played the bloody cello? Now, wasn't that too richly bizarre? They must have had wonderful musical evenings together.

He knew he was taking a bit of a risk, going to the concert, but he couldn't sit calmly back at the caravan park, slumming it while his wife and her lover were part of a concert in the town. Not that he would hear the music! But it would be fun watching them.

His face abruptly twisted itself into fury. No way was Laura getting away with it. She'd never run from him again.

The concert was going to be very successful. Apparently the whole bloody town had turned out. It was as crowded as an opening night at a city theatre. Surely they couldn't actually be interested in classical music? Beethoven. Schubert. And something else on the programme. A local guy. Alex Matheson.

That'd be good, he thought with weary contempt. He didn't care. This lot were just making the best of what was on offer. He hunched himself in a back seat, all nerves and quivering anger. People glanced at him. After a while he remembered he ought to nod and maybe give a smile here and there.

An hour and a half passed, during which his stomach churned so much he felt like rushing out of the theatre and being ill. The old girl he'd seen at the house was one of the quintet. And treacherous Laura, looking absolutely beautiful in a long black skirt of ribboned lace with one of her glittering little tops, sat at the piano, fingers running up and down with brilliance, full of music.

Damn her! Pulses were beating a rhythm in his head like one of those old military band marches. He turned his attention again to Kellerman. Big guy. He looked as if he'd have bone-crushing strength. Until this moment he'd thought playing a musical instrument wasn't manly, but this guy laid that idea to rest. He was damned good. The whole ensemble was damned good. He had expected the recital to be pathetic.

Before the deafening applause was over he got quickly
away. He'd left his vehicle in a side street. He felt stupid.
Almost bested. Badly shaken by what he had seen and heard.
He had a career. A reputation. His peers considered him brilliant. There was no place in his life for violence. Except he
wanted Laura back.

Harriet had organised the supper—marvellous food—everyone was on a high, enjoying themselves immensely, mixing
with all the locals who had been invited.

"I feel so much like celebrating!" Harriet cried warmly,
her manner so vivacious she might have received a light elec-
tric shock. She put an affectionate arm around Laura's waist.
"We're so proud of you, Laura. It isn't always easy settling
into a group, but you've done wonderfully well. So in possession of your instrument, and such a lovely touch! I think
we did extremely well. So does the audience, apparently. I
take it you've told Evan about you know who?" she whispered, leaning her head closer.

"I have." Laura smiled.

"How did he take it? Forgive me for being an old busy-
body, but I have to know."

"He was appalled, Harriet. First of all that I had a husband.
But then when I told him all about the ruins of my marriage
he forgave me. He's determined to go to Brisbane and confront Colin. I can't stop him. He won't listen and he insists
he doesn't want me there. At first anyway."

"Probably he's got a point," Harriet considered.

"I'll be starting divorce proceedings as soon as possible
after that."

"And marrying Evan, my dear?" Harriet's grey eyes were
full of sympathy and interest. "Seeing you both together, I
can't believe it's just an affair."

"I love him, Harriet, and he loves me."

"The most beautiful words in the world. You both have
to get on with your lives."

"I don't want you to go in the morning." They were
inside the house and she was speaking very softly, almost
whispering.

"We've discussed this, Laura," he said firmly, picking her up in his arms and carrying her through to the bedroom.

"I don't want you to go on your own."

"And I don't want you there, my darling, when I confront him. You'll have your turn. I'd like to see to Dr Colin Morcombe privately. It's one thing to terrorize a woman, and quite another to try the same tactics on a man. I'd be quite happy to slap him around a bit so he knows how it feels."

"He certainly needs it, but that might rebound on you in some way. He's very vindictive. He'd say and do almost anything to cause you harm."

"We'll see about that," Evan said grimly.

"You might find it difficult to reach him. He has people fronting for him. Staff."

"You just leave that to me," Evan said, fiercely despising the man Laura had married. "For now I want to make love to you. Okay?"

"Perfect. I'm terribly terribly sorry I married Colin. I only want you."

"That's why I have to get things settled," he said, gently starting to undress her. "What sort of a man is he to willingly and brutally abuse you? A doctor too. It's beyond imagining. I don't fancy he'll want the story to get around, or people wondering where he got his black eye."

"You wouldn't!"

"My darling, I'm going to make him perfectly well aware of what might happen to him if he dares approach you again," Evan said, very crisply.

He reached out a hand to caress her—just a brush of the skin, yet it sent desire rippling all over her.

This was Evan's great gift to her. This wonderful sense of herself as a woman.

CHAPTER FOURTEEN

IT WAS going to be a very long day, Laura thought. Evan by now would be at the heliport, awaiting his connection for the long flight to Brisbane.

He'd already called ahead to make sure Colin was at his city practice, inventing a story about needing urgent medical attention. Dr Romsey, Doctor Morcombe's partner, had a cancellation the following day, he'd been told. Would Dr Romsey do? No, Evan insisted. He was coming a long way to see Dr Morcombe on excellent recommendation.

The truth. There was something urgent to be dealt with. Still, she wished he'd let her go along with him all the same. She wouldn't be able to stop worrying until he got back. It wasn't easy dealing with a man who was sick in the head. That was how she thought of Colin. Sick in the head. And because of it very dangerous.

It was everywhere, his threat: I'll never let you go.

How far would he go to keep her? Evan was an experienced man, big and powerful. A man who had lived through many dangers. He would be able to handle Colin, she comforted herself. Colin wouldn't be so shockingly aggressive with Evan around. Neither could Colin afford a scandal. His parents would hate it. They might even consider censuring their son. Laura flipped back and forth with the positives and the negatives until she heard a rap on the back door.

No one came the back way, she thought in surprise. Then she remembered a woman who made excellent jams and preserves sometimes left her car in the vacant allotment to the rear of the cottage when she worked the area.

With her darling little Freddy purring happily in her arms, Laura went to the door. She was already smiling as she opened it, standing back framed in the doorway.

For an instant she had a sensation of being separated from

her own body. Her eyes were wide open, yet she felt she might be in the middle of a nightmare.

Colin! She understood the deadly seriousness immediately.

"Having a good time in Koomera Crossing, are we, darling?" he asked with a sinister smile.

She might be fooling herself, but she no longer felt completely at his mercy. "Get right away from here, Colin," she warned with considerable fire. "This is my home."

The anger in her voice and body alerting Freddy to the fact that the visitor wasn't welcome. Instead of high-tailing it out through the back door, the kitten flew for Colin's chest, claws digging in so sharply Colin gave an involuntary yelp.

"Bloody thing!" His face contorted as he tried unsuccessfully to fling Freddy away. Only Freddy was no longer a sweet little kitten, but the complete cat ready for a scrap. "Bloody thing scratched me," Colin howled in amazement, continuing to wrestle the kitten until finally he managed to rip it from his shirt and throw it forcibly outside.

"Did you have to do that?" Laura watched the kitten collapse, then struggle up.

"Boy, have you got problems," he chided. "Listen to you. All up in arms about a cat."

"How did you get here, Colin?" Laura stood her ground. "You're supposed to be in Brisbane."

"Ah, yes! That worked just like I thought it would." He pushed her so hard she had to clutch at something to prevent herself from falling. "I told my staff not to give out any information to the contrary. Good thinking, eh?" He gave her the familiar look of triumph. "So your lover went rushing off, delivering you nicely into my hands. Bitch!" He reached out a long arm and slapped her so hard across the face she thought her neck would snap.

Were more calamities coming? She shook her head to clear it, nonetheless realizing she wasn't as physically afraid of him. Evan had taught her a few karate moves. She could use them.

Colin kicked the door shut, then turned the lock. "Nothing to protect you now, Laura." He glanced around like a predatory hawk. "This place is disgusting. A joke! How you can live in it I can't imagine. Are you sure you haven't totally lost it?"

"It's heaven without you, Colin," she assured him, wondering the next move to make. If the worst came to the worst there was a lock on her bedroom door and she could cry for help from the window. "By the way, that's a terrible disguise?"

"Definitely not me." He smirked. "But I needed to move around without being noticed. I do attract attention, as you know. I was at the concert last night. You were very good. And so was Kellerman. Quite a surprise, though I didn't give you any applause. How was Ayers Rock?"

Laura wondered when the rage was coming. How she would cope with it. "None of your business."

"Are you serious? You're my wife."

"Not for much longer. I want a divorce, Colin."

Now the arctic eyes flared. "You might be a rotten wife, but there's no divorce." There was a strange finality in his tone. "We need to be together. That's what makes my life work."

"You mean you need someone to torment." Laura saw her chance. She moved very quickly, darting into the kitchen. The counter was between them, with its drawer full of knives. "I'm never coming back to you, Colin."

"Of course you are." He turned on another smile for her. "You made a lifetime commitment, darling, remember?"

"Your actions changed that." Laura took strength from the fact that her voice was quite calm.

"Trying to prove how brave we are, are we?" He snaked out an arm for her but she backed away.

"I have friends in this town, Colin. Even with Evan gone I have people who will come to my aid."

"Possession is nine-tenths of the law, darling," he reminded her. "They won't find you here, anyway. You won't be allowed to yell for help either, if that's what you're considering. You're my wife, Laura. Doesn't that mean anything to you?"

"It stopped meaning anything to me on my honeymoon," Laura countered, her expression full of condemnation. "I made a terrible choice in life with you, Colin. You're vicious. A cruel bully who used me, a woman, your wife, for a punching bag. I think that makes you a gutless wonder. And you're a man who's supposed to be devoting his life to caring for people. That's something your colleagues really should hear. How your wife got to know the inner workings of a psychopath. I bet I don't have to tell your mother either. I've seen the worry in her eyes."

"You leave my mother out of this," he rasped, the familiar glare in his eyes.

"When she realizes what you've done, Colin, she might turn her back on you."

"As if she'd believe you over me," he said coldly, although his handsome features were distorted with anger.

"I think my lawyers might be able to wring the truth out of you, Colin," Laura said very quietly. "You see, it's all over. God is giving me a second chance."

"God is?" His voice rose comically. "You don't seem to understand, Laura. God is on my side. Our marriage was made in heaven. I'm your husband. I'm not letting you go."

"There are rules, Colin, even you have to obey," she continued, using the same quiet, reasoning tone. "I'm free under the law. You mightn't appreciate a scandal. I'll make one if I have to. You can count on that."

"And *you* can count on something happening to Kellerman." His face and voice assumed a blaze of menace.

"What are we talking? Murder? I wouldn't put it past you. But you wouldn't do it with your own precious hands. You'd find some career criminal."

He nodded, as though there was nothing unusual about what she was saying. "I see it as a legitimate way to get rid of a rival. All's fair in love and war, don't they say? There are people who'll do anything for a price."

"So there are, but they usually go to jail."

"My darling, I'd go to jail before I let Kellerman have you," he said simply. "Now, don't make me furious," he advised, with another malicious smile. "Pack a few things and throw them in a bag. Leave a little note for your so-called friends saying you're going off exploring with a friend. We're getting out of here."

He'd all but broken her once. He wasn't going to do it again. "Sorry, Colin," she said. "That's not about to happen. You're the one getting out of here. Not me, you monster!"

Unable to contain herself, Laura picked up a pottery bowl that usually held fruit, throwing it with some force.

"Goodness me!" he scoffed, though the bowl had found its target, grazing his temple before shattering on the tiles. "Isn't this just the perfect time for you to find a little guts? Are we going to have a big fight? I'm one hundred per cent sure who'll win. Don't be a fool, Laura. I don't want to hit you, but you always provoke me. Do as I say now. Make it quick. I'm itching to be out of here."

"I bet!" Laura muttered, feeling a strange sense of detachment. "It's all got to stop now, Colin. I'd rather die than live my life with you."

"Never say that!" he snarled, endeavouring to corner her, but she took off in the direction of her bedroom, where she planned to yell like hell.

"No need to die, Laura." He came after her with his long stride, tugging viciously at her flying mane of hair, using it as a rope to jerk her back to him. "We'll work something out." His breath fanned her cheek; his hand sought her breast. "I love you. I do. I never feel the excitement except with you."

"You're mad!" She was fighting in earnest now.

"You made me mad. I wasn't always like this."

"Oh, yes, you were. I bet you tortured little animals. Cut them up. Let go, you cowardly bastard!" She struggled wildly, but to no effect.

How do I stop him? How do I stop him? The little bit of training she'd had was turning out to be useless against his superior strength. That got to her. She kicked and kicked, but his surgeon's hands were like steel claws, ripping at her hair, ripping at her clothing.

This wasn't going to happen. It all fitted together now. He was obsessed with her. In desperation she screamed, "Evan!" though she knew Evan was hundreds of miles away by now.

"Shut up!" There was an electrifying anger in his voice, and an edge of panic too. She had never been this hard to subdue, but he'd come equipped with the answer. He was a doctor after all. Pain shot through his shin as she kicked back at him. He gave a low growl, cruelly cuffing her with one hand and removing his glove with the other.

"Someone please help me!" Laura shrieked, her heart hammering in her chest. Oh, God, surely someone would hear? Hadn't she suffered enough at Colin's hands? She caught a strong whiff of some chemical or other. It was coming off a bandage or white pad he wore beneath his glove.

She felt horror. Ether? Chloroform? Which one had the odour? What did it matter? Before she could figure it out his hands clamped down hard over her nose and mouth. "You really are a naughty girl!"

She fought harder, determined she wasn't going to stop, but her brain was turning fuzzy. She tried to jerk her head away, knowing he was going to abduct her. She couldn't give up the fight...couldn't...

Somehow she managed to twist her body side-on, hoping she could aim a good kick at his groin.

"Bitch!" He cuffed her again, viciously, getting the pad back into position over her nose and mouth.

She was going to black out.

Evan, I tried.

He scarcely had a minute to bundle her up before he heard a car door slam.

"God!" The very air around him started to roar. Nothing and no one was going to get in his way.

He left her lying on the floor, making a rush to the front window to stare out. Incredibly, the caller was Kellerman. Very large. Well muscled. Very strong. He'd need a weapon to stop him.

Colin's eyes whizzed around swiftly, spotted the very

thing. A heavy brass ornament. That should put a dent in Kellerman's skull. He took up a position behind the door. Every pulse was hammering. This wasn't supposed to happen.

The bastard had a key. A key to his wife's miserable little cottage. Hell, the last person on earth he'd expected was Kellerman. What had brought him back? And surely Laura had made a sound?

He turned his head briefly, ears straining. She shouldn't have made a sound unless the strength of the anaesthetic had dissipated beneath his glove.

In the ringing silence Colin Morcombe got ready to strike, only Kellerman was ready for him.

Incredible! He must have received some warning. This couldn't be happening, he thought, his rage surging. He'd planned it all perfectly, every step. Nothing could go wrong. Yet for a terrifying minute he was hurtling across the room, smashing into the wall.

The man was unbelievably strong. Colin was actually powerless to get up. The realization called forth unfamiliar humiliation. He was meant to win.

"Morcombe, is it?" Evan stood over the cowering figure on the floor, loathing what he saw. Smooth and handsome, like a reptile, died black hair slicked back. "Where's Laura?" he demanded, wanting to hurl Morcombe again.

"She's not ready to talk to you right now," Morcombe said, and incredibly smiled.

"Laura?" Evan called, unable to keep the fear and urgency out of his voice. "If you've hurt her, God help you." He sucked in a harsh breath.

"You're talking about my wife, Kellerman. *My* wife, not yours." Colin's voice dripped with irony.

"The one you were supposed to love and cherish?" Evan reached down powerfully to grab Morcombe's collar, dragging him clear across the hallway with one furious tug.

"You can't want that stupid little bitch? She's a pathological liar. She's got problems. Ask her about her father. He was the abuser, not me."

"Shut up, you screwed-up bastard," Evan warned, feeling a terrible violence against this man. "Don't talk your poison to me." Now Evan could see Laura's crumpled up body. "Oh, God, what have you done to her?" He dragged the reptile up. This wasn't a man.

"She's just taking a little nap. Trust me." There was sheer hatred in Colin's eyes.

"Then why don't you do the same?" Unable to prevent himself, Evan smashed his fist into Morcombe's jaw, a light-ning-swift punch that made Morcombe's head snap sharply to one side. He staggered backwards, then collapsed. Beaten.

"Laura?" Feeling the cold hand of horror, Evan rushed to her, his body suddenly bathed in a cold sweat. He dropped to his knees, feeling for her pulse. Slow. The bastard had drugged her. He caught a whiff of something. Ether? My God! Clearly Morcombe had gone over the edge with his obsession for his wife. Her shirt was torn, buttons ripped away.

"Laura, Laura," he whispered in agony, and was heart-ened beyond belief to hear a tiny moan come from her lips. She was coming round. Having seen so much violence, his aversion to it was on record. But he felt like reducing Morcombe the wife-beater to pulp.

Tenderly Evan got his arms beneath Laura, lifting her from the floor. Clever, observant Harriet! Her hunch, premoni-tion—whatever had got him back. It would take a lifetime to thank her. He placed Laura on the sofa, rubbing both her hands. The front door was still open, so there was plenty of fresh air streaming through the door,

"Oh, my sweet, sweet girl!" She looked especially small, and now he could see clearly that she had abrasions on her cheek and the beginnings of a black eye.

That did it. He stood up precipitately, his back towards where he had left Morcombe lying. He took one blow after another as Morcombe recovered and whirred into action.

"God damn you to hell!" Evan swung around, outraged, not even feeling the punches. Morcombe had picked the wrong man. He was only dangerous to women. Yet there was madness in those artic blue eyes. And in the midst of his fury Evan felt tremendous shock Morcombe, a skilled surgeon, had chosen this way.

Though her vision was blurry Laura saw her husband's attack on Evan. She didn't stop to marvel why Evan was there. He just was. An answer to her prayers. She wobbled up, staggered badly, almost fell over but righted her balance, telling herself to go, *go*, to Evan's rescue.

"I'm coming!" she shouted, or she thought she shouted. There was a strange underwater sensation in her ears.

Hearing her dazed voice, Evan slowed down his systematic pummelling, twisting his head to her. "Laura, go back. Phone the police if you can."

Given such a welcome distraction, Colin didn't hesitate to land a few more blows on his powerful opponent. He had never imagined himself in a fist fight with another man. As unpleasant as hell!

"Monster!" Laura cried. All she could think of was getting to Evan. Evan needed her, she thought woozily, though surely it was Colin who was bleeding, blood trickling from his nose to his mouth and chin.

Her fingers closed around something on the sideboard. A weapon at last.

As quickly as she could, which was in reality slow motion, she reached out and with the greatest effort whacked her abusive husband on the head.

"That'll take care of him!" she said with satisfaction, before her rubbery legs gave out from under her.

Colin showed no signs of disagreeing. He showed no signs of getting up either, though it was moments before Laura allowed Evan to take the weapon from her hand.

They waited precisely three minutes after Evan's phone call for Constable Pat Barratt to arrive, closely followed up by Harriet Crompton.

"It was Harriet who tipped me off," Evan told Laura thankfully, as a very hostile Colin stood as still as a stone statue while the constable handcuffed him.

Colin's colour rose alarmingly. "I'm a respected surgeon," he said hoarsely, his cold, handsome face grey with shock. "A gentleman. A man of status. This is an outrage. A gentleman like me to have his hands handcuffed behind his back— You're making a great mistake, Officer. It was Kellerman who assaulted me. I'll bring charges."

"I'm the one who'll be pressing charges, Colin," Laura said in a near cheerful voice.

"Don't dare try," he told her through gritted teeth.

"She will," Evan confirmed. "You may as well take him away, Pat, and thank you for coming so promptly." Evan nodded to the constable, who nodded back.

"No worries. That's my job."

"Don't think this is the last you'll be hearing from me," Colin threatened, obviously finding his position intolerable. "I'm the victim here." He looked and acted as though he truly believed it.

"I wouldn't be making threats, sir, if I were you." Constable Barratt warned, in a calm, civil voice. "You're in enough trouble as it is. We take your behaviour very seriously out here. Assault. Deprivation of liberty. The use of an anaesthetic to subdue. All serious, sir. When you're ready, Laura, you and Evan might come down to the station and make a statement."

"Will do, Pat, and many thanks."

"My goodness, I do believe I was on the verge of a heart attack," Harriet said some time later, having made that great restorative pot of tea, with plenty of sugar.

"So that was your husband." She made a few little clicking noises with her tongue. "It must have been the good Lord who warned me. I first spied him hanging around the cottage a few days ago. He waited for me to go, then he doubled back. Then I saw him ducking out of the concert. Something clicked in my head. I sensed trouble. I was sure he wasn't to be trusted. Then when I saw him driving into town this morning I thought, That's no stranger in town, that's Laura's husband. I played my hunch and contacted Evan immediately. I've always had a good nose for sniffing out trouble."

"After today you won't get either of us to disagree," Evan said with wry affection.

"Do you think we've got rid of him?" Harriet shuddered. Having seen the man, and those mad eyes, she couldn't bear to think what Laura had endured.

"Definitely," Evan answered. "He's nothing but a vicious woman-abuser. Laura has me to stand with her now." He drew Laura closer to his side, looking down at her with pride and love. "You're a brave woman. You know that?"

"I am with you around." Laura smiled back into his loving eyes.

"I'm not taking all the credit." Evan grinned. "You got in the king hit. You don't have to worry any more, my love. 'Gentleman' Morcombe—can you beat that? He was calling himself a gentleman—is nothing now. Probably his career is in tatters, but he has no one to blame but himself. Like Pat said, he's in a lot of trouble."

"I almost feel sorry for him," Laura said.

"Don't. He doesn't deserve it."

"Of course he doesn't." Laura put her arms around Evan, hugging him tightly. "My hero!"

"Husband would sound a million times sweeter," Evan responded, dropping a kiss on her temple

"Wouldn't it ever!" Harriet exclaimed in high delight, and gave them the thumbs up. "Really, you know, I'd like to manage your wedding reception," she said with her characteristic directness.

"Why not!" Laura and Evan spoke together.

Nothing but elation.

EPILOGUE

Fourteen months later

VENICE was gorgeous. For a whole month they wandered everywhere, succumbing to its fabled beauty.

They revelled in its sights, its sounds, its smells, the way the sun glittered on the murky turquoise water of the lagoon. They took dozens of gondola rides, and from the water gazed out on the marble and stone palaces and churches walling the Grand Canal that wound through the city heart. They slipped under the stone Rialto Bridge, the wooden bridge at the Accademia, and got out at St Mark's Square, the centre of tourist activity.

The Cathedral of Saint Mark, on the east side of the square, was a wonderful example of Byzantine architecture, the Campanile—a bell tower—standing nearby. Just off the Square was the pink and white fairy floss of the Doges Palace, residence of the early Venetian rulers.

They tried in their enchantment to take in all this city of legend had to offer, but there was so little time. The priceless artworks on display throughout Venice they devoured: the Academy of Fine Arts, Titian, Tintoretto, Veronese. They strolled at dusk along the waterfront, watching the buoys on the water light up like lanterns, waiting for a vaporetto to come to take them on yet another mystery journey.

They dined out at famous restaurants. Stayed at a lovely private apartment lent to them by a friend of Evan's. At night they slept wrapped in each other's arms.

Rapture!

In the morning they woke to the sun streaming into their bedroom, because they didn't bother to close the shutters. This was their honeymoon. They had waited a full year for Laura's divorce to come through and now they were man and

180

wife. Sharing their blissful life. Day after day. Week after week. Each minute brought them more joy, more intimacy.

On their last evening they walked hand in hand through the square of San Marco, listening to the babble of languages around them, the voices of excited children, the music the water made, splashing and lapping against stone.

"Venice has been everything I ever read about it," Laura said dreamily, snuggling into the warmth of her husband.

"It's like Paris. It never disappoints." Evan smiled down at her.

"It's been fantastic." Laura lifted her head to inhale the peculiar odour of the city, a kind of lemony-limey freshness mixed with the dankness of brackish water. "The two of us together. How can I ever tell you how wonderful it's been, my husband?"

"You'll have a lifetime to do it." He embraced her, pressing her against him. "My wife, my lovely Laura." On a wave of euphoria he bent his head over her, kissing her passionately, while Laura, freed of all constraint by his love, responded in kind.

Both of them were oblivious to the little wave of clapping from people who strolled benignly by.

Venice was the city for lovers.

"Tomorrow we begin our journey home," Evan said as they walked on.

"Home. Isn't that a wonderful word?" she rounded her lips on it. "All this has been wonderful. We could never spend enough time here. But I'm missing the world we left. Its sheer vastness and mystery. We have so much open space. And I miss our friends. They've been so good to us. Do you think we'll stay in Koomera Crossing? Your book, now that it's finished, is so good. It's expected to do very well. Maybe you could become a writer full time? It's something you enjoy."

"I've thought about it," he admitted. In fact he had lots of ideas he could pursue.

"I could compose," she said sweetly. "There's music all

around us. I feel so happy, so focused—I know I could get the sounds in my head down on paper.''

''I'm sure you could,'' he answered, very proud of her. ''That piece you wrote for your father is truly beautiful. Mother thought so too. It's a great joy to me you two clicked so wonderfully well. I knew you would.''

Laura's smile was full of charm. ''Your mother is a beautiful woman in every way. I'll never forget how happy she was at our wedding. How she played for us. It brought such peace and calm to have her there. My mother and Craig. Everyone getting on so well. Our wedding day was the most perfect day of my life.''

''And mine.'' He bent to kiss her, an expression of great happiness lighting his strongly hewn face. ''Let's wait a while and see where life takes us. We're together. We have one another. Sometimes I think I want nothing else but the two of us. Then again, I expect I'll have a family to support...''

That sent sparkles of joy rushing through her. She smiled, blushed and nodded. ''I feel we mightn't have to wait all that much longer,'' she told him in a voice that was lyrical in its joy.

His hand was instantly at her shoulder. Such a look of wonderment on his face. He thought he loved her so much his heart could barely contain it.

''What does that mean, sweetheart?'' Surrounded by people, he only had eyes and ears for her.

She looked up at him and laughed. The most radiant feeling of contentment was taking possession of her. Every day of her life with him she was falling deeper and deeper in love.

''I'll know for sure by the time we get home,'' she promised.

Read over for a preview of
Outback Bridegroom.
Coming soon in Koomera Crossing
from Margaret Way.

CHRISTINE! If he lived to be a hundred, received a message of congratulations from the Queen, he doubted he could ever forget his old pal Christine, who these days wouldn't give him the time of day.

It had been a long hike for Chris, from awkward adolescent, head ducking, shoulders slouching in an effort to hide her height, to fêted international model who regularly bagged the cover of *Vogue*, *Harper's Bazaar* and the like. And the first moment he'd laid eyes on her in years she was walking with immense style—all that catwalk training hadn't gone to waste—down Wunnamurra's grand divided staircase.

Wow, what a knockout!

"Mitchell, how lovely to see you again!" Her stunning face turned on the now famous smile. "It's so good of you to come."

"Hey, we're family aren't we, Chrissy?" He sauntered up to her, didn't attempt to hug her, or kiss her cheek. He settled for a sardonic handshake. She wouldn't like the Chrissy, but he just wanted to let her know he'd never settle for the usual baloney. "Lovely to see you" didn't true after the way she'd treated him.

She was so beautiful he could hardly bear the sight of her. Enid's "ugly duckling" had long since turned into a swan. He'd always known she would. In her adolescence Enid and her grandmother, Ruth, had hardly had a kind word to say to Chris regarding her coltish, somewhat androgynous look, the insouciant "boy" in her jodhpurs and shirts. Of course she'd cultivated the look deliberately in retaliation.

In those days Christine had been like a creature of the wild trapped in a cage. She had fled her unhappy home. Anyone who'd had anything to do with Enid and Ruth could understand that. Except she had fled him when he had thought they were never more in love.

Now Ruth McQueen's death had brought Christine home…

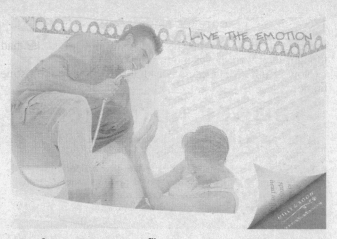

Modern Romance™
...seduction and
passion guaranteed

Tender Romance™
...love affairs that
last a lifetime

Medical Romance™
...medical drama
on the pulse

Historical Romance™
...rich, vivid and
passionate

Sensual Romance™
...sassy, sexy and
seductive

Blaze Romance™
...the temperature's
rising

27 new titles every month.

Live the emotion

MILLS & BOON®

Invitations to Seduction

THREE SIZZLING STORIES FROM TODAY'S HOTTEST WRITERS!

VICKI LEWIS THOMPSON
CARLY PHILLIPS · JANELLE DENISON

Available from 15th August 2003

*Available at most branches of WH Smith,
Tesco, Martins, Borders, Eason, Sainsbury's
and all good paperback bookshops.*

0903/024/MB79

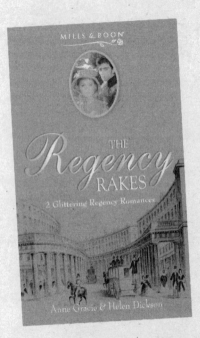

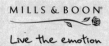

MILLS & BOON®

Live the emotion

PENNINGTON

Catherine George

PENNINGTON

Earthbound Angel

MILLS & BOON

BOOK THREE

Available from 5th September 2003

*Available at most branches of WHSmith, Tesco, Martins, Borders,
Eason, Sainsbury's, and most good paperback bookshops.*

FREE!

4 Books
and a surprise gift!

We would like to take this opportunity to thank you for reading this Mills & Boon® book by offering you the chance to take FOUR more specially selected titles from the Tender Romance™ series absolutely FREE! We're also making this offer to introduce you to the benefits of the Reader Service™ —

- ★ FREE home delivery
- ★ FREE gifts and competitions
- ★ FREE monthly Newsletter
- ★ Books available before they're in the shops
- ★ Exclusive Reader Service discount

Accepting these FREE books and gift places you under no obligation to buy; you may cancel at any time, even after receiving your free shipment. Simply complete your details below and return the entire page to the address below. *You don't even need a stamp!*

YES! Please send me 4 free Tender Romance books and a surprise gift. I understand that unless you hear from me, I will receive 6 superb new titles every month for just £2.60 each, postage and packing free. I am under no obligation to purchase any books and may cancel my subscription at any time. The free books and gift will be mine to keep in any case.

N3ZEF

Ms/Mrs/Miss/Mr ....Initials..
BLOCK CAPITALS PLEASE

Surname..

Address...

....

....Postcode ....

Send this whole page to:
UK: The Reader Service, FREEPOST CN81, Croydon, CR9 3WZ
EIRE: The Reader Service, PO Box 4546, Kilcock, County Kildare (stamp required)